we were one once

book 2

Books by Willow Madison

True Nature

True Beginnings

True Choices

True Control 4.1

True Control 4.2

we were one once 1

Existential Angst

the SAYER

we were one once

book 2

Willow Madison

Madison, Willow

we were one once (One, Book Two)

Front Cover Design by David Colon (www.colonfilm.com); Back Cover Design by XIX (www.thenineteen.net)

Edit by Q (www.editingbyq.com)

This is a work of fiction. Names, characters, places and incidents are either the product of the author's imagination or are used fictitiously, and any resemblance to actual persons, living or dead, business establishments, events or locales is entirely coincidental.

This book is intended for adults only. Spanking and other sexual activities represented in this book are fantasies only, intended for adults. Nothing in the book should be interpreted as advocating any non-consensual spanking activity or the spanking of minors.

www.willowmadisonbooks.com

ISBN-13: 978-0-9963191-6-4
ISBN-10: 0-9963191-6-6

Prologue

Where is your ancient courage?
You were used to say extremities was the trier of spirits;
That common chances common men could bear;
That when the sea was calm all boats alike showed
mastership in floating.
- William Shakespeare

I float on the edge, half in, half out, stretched, motionless. The stars stare blankly back at me. The full moon is on its way for Lilly's promise.

This is the last of my thoughts before I give in to the calmness, the emptiness. I don't feel the pain. I never do.

I feel the love. I feel the need. I let these waves wash over me, waves you create with your reach for me.

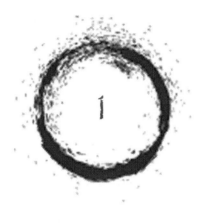

1

Anderson Valley: Simon Lamb

"Welcome to my home, Miles." I reach to shake the man's hand, and his darkly hooded eyes finally meet mine. He seems to be trying to assess me in some way, shaking hands a little too long and firm for the standard niceties. I instinctively don't like him, and his gaze keeps darting to Red behind me. I can't ignore his appraisal of her as his stare continues to shift away from me. Cary remains smiling at us, oblivious to the heavy silence in the room.

"Pleasure's all mine, Mr. Lamb. I've heard so much about you." And I've heard nothing about you, but I keep this to myself. No point in being rude. Yet. It's my cousin that deserves his ass kicked for this intrusion.

I turn away from Miles to introduce Red; really, it's to give her a warning look to stay away from this guy. "This is Scarlet." I can see that she's in trouble, and it's not because I'm calling her by the stupid name I made up to use in front of my cousin either.

She stands with her usual angles jutting out, her long red dress highlighting her slender sharpness, but she is inexplicably changed. It's not the change I've come to anticipate with her identity switches either—not the sand shifting under her smooth exterior into a new state of being kind of change. No, she's still Red but frozen—sand locked behind glass now, only a reflection of her without the usual fieriness.

Standing near the piano, she's locked in place, lost in this no man's land of non-expression. I move towards her, but she stays blank. I take her hand, and she slowly pulls her eyes to mine. Her beautiful dark eyes, so lively and flirtatious only moments before, now barely spark to life at the contact.

I recognize this as her trick of retreating into the safety of her own head just enough to not fully feel something. Grace had explained that it's like being on a stage. All five personalities can be there at once or only one, but whichever identity is center stage can step back "out of the light," is how she put it. I've become familiar with this diffused look over the last month, with all of her subtle looks and changes, but it's still a mystery to me how it all works exactly.

There is a scant scent of fear masking her usual spiciness now too. This makes my heart race. Red isn't afraid of anything. I should know. I've shown her more of my depraved, sick mind than any one woman has ever seen. She's been my match every time. Seeing her afraid now, I have that jealousy induced shooting pain to my stomach again, quickly followed by concern for her mental state.

I frown, but she doesn't respond with anything except more impassive blinking. Suddenly, my large grand hall seems too small, filled with too many people. I'm definitely kicking Cary's ass tonight for this.

"Scarlet?" Miles' voice is silk gliding over velvet. It grates on my nerves. He comes closer to us and puts his hand out, taking Red's other hand and bringing it to his lips. I watch this, fighting the urge to punch his pompous face for thinking he can touch her. I allow my years of living discreetly to stop me from taking my fists to this asshole. For now. "A greater pleasure I could not imagine, my dear."

Red manages to come out of her freeze a little more, snatching her hand away from Miles. That's my girl. She always seems to understand what I think and feel, even before I do. Fucking annoying sometimes. Right now, I'm glad that she can read my increased anger and jealousy so easily.

She doesn't meet my eyes, though, and avoids the glare I'm shooting at her, then him. Red only moves away from us and takes a seat on the piano bench.

Cary jumps into the awkwardness. "Miles was introduced to me by Bradford last week, Simon. He thought you two might be able to come to terms." He knows my rule of only taking clients that are known to me. I've sold several products to Bradford over the years, but that doesn't excuse Cary for bringing a stranger into my home and without warning.

I take my eyes off Red long enough to give a few dagger looks in my cousin's direction. "I'm retiring." His shocked face is almost worth it. His eyes go so round they're more white than blue. I ignore this and turn again to my unwelcome guest. "So, you'll have to resource your product needs from someone else, Miles. I may be able to give you a recommendation though." I want this man out of my house as quickly as possible. I need to attend to Red, see what's got her so rattled.

This is the first episode of her withdrawing like this since we came to our strange understanding a month ago. I've been fearing what would happen if she lost control of her batshit nuttiness. Tonight of all nights is not good. I don't want to have to explain too much to Cary. And I haven't had enough time to get my head around what all this really means for us. *Us*. Fuck.

Miles only smiles at me with a bland look, like I didn't just brush him off. "I was hoping to talk business in private, Mr. Lamb." He shifts his eyes to Red again, who's still sitting in her semi-frozen state. His eyes linger on her longer than I like. Fuck. I really need to get control of this jealousy shit. How do normal people handle this?

"That'll have to wait then. We're late for a concert and dinner." I glance at Cary. He's still recovering his shocked look, but he nods at me. He's not an idiot. He understands that he's pissed me off tonight. He doesn't know why, but that doesn't matter. He's quick to respond to my subtle nod towards the door.

Cary puts his hand out, directing Miles back towards my foyer. "I'm sure we can be in touch in the next couple of days."

But Miles doesn't move towards the door. He stays in the same spot, ignoring Cary, ignoring me. Instead, this fucker turns to Red and addresses her with a more commanding tone. "Play for me." He nods towards the piano in front of her.

I answer for Red tersely, "She doesn't play," moving to block his view of her.

I square my already tense shoulders and take a closer look at the man. Miles Vanderson isn't known to me. The fact that my cousin would bring him here unannounced is not a good sign. Cary knows better. Bradford will have some explaining to do too. I don't like surprises. I especially don't like them in my home.

Miles is maybe an inch or two taller than me, but he doesn't come close to matching my physical strength. His expensive suit does nothing to hide his athletic build though. He seems purposely older than his age—a practiced way of looking and talking. He's obviously a man who's used to getting what he wants through intimidation. That shit won't fly with me.

His dark hair is kept very short and his darker eyes are large and piercing with intensity. He appears casual enough, comfortable; but my years of watching people, assessing strengths and weaknesses, tell me that his casualness is forced. Miles is restraining himself, uncomfortable being here. Maybe he's not used to dealing with someone like me, on unfamiliar ground talking about acquiring a woman to be his slave? He doesn't seem hesitant though, and he didn't look away as Cary introduced us. And he hasn't stopped eyeing Red like she's prime fucking beef and he's a vegan off the wagon.

My thoughts are interrupted by music behind me. Cary and Miles move to watch Red. I turn slowly and correct myself. It's Grace who's playing my piano. She's not just playing; she's good actually. I didn't know she could. She hasn't even stood near it until tonight.

Of course, I don't know a lot about her, and what I do know is more shocking than learning that she's a modestly good pianist. After spending four weeks together, every minute of every day, I still don't know her real name even or what happened in her past to shatter her into five separate pieces. I have my theories, but she won't open up to me about anything before two years ago when she came to San Francisco. I've tried getting info out of Red and Grace, but both are stubborn in their own ways. Neither lets their guard down, not even in bed.

I'm startled awake by her fingertips dancing lightly up my stomach. I'm chilled now from the sweat that still clings to us, but I have my breath back at least. I must've only dozed off for a few minutes. The overhead light is still dimmed, and the sheets are cold as I move.

I return her sweet smile up to me, pulling her hand to my lips and kissing her fingers softly. "Hello, Grace." She beams. All of her versions seem so pleased when I recognize the change between them so easily. A smile that big just for me pleases me too.

I'd fallen asleep with Red in my arms, our panting the perfect melody to put me into a post-sex slumber that would've lasted all night. I can see by the blush on Grace's cheeks that she has other ideas.

I roll into her, propping my head up on my crooked elbow. My fingers trace absently over her nipples, my eyes wandering down her stretched body. She lies perfectly still under my inspection of her, waiting and looking up at me with her eyes large.

I went light on Red tonight, just a feathering with a flogger that only left a few pink spots on her body. The sweat and panting came from the number of times we brought each other to climax, even without the usual intricate roping and whippings. I'd closed my eyes thinking that it'd be days before I would have the energy for sex again.

I guess I was wrong. Watching Grace shiver and move with my light touch is enough to stir my need for her. "Be still. No movement unless it's one I order." She relaxes into the bed more, melting into my touch. She loves when I take charge of her.

I've learned the difference between Red and Grace in bed. What they like and don't like is very different—mind-bogglingly different—and I'm feeling the familiar guilt at thinking of one while with the other. It's an insanity that makes me harder.

With Red, it's all about exploring limits. We haven't found any yet. Every position, every implement, every twisted way I can think—she pushes for more. Her *submission isn't so much given to me as one I earn each time.*

When I think I can't push her further, when she's had enough, she always gets this look in her eyes. It's the look I think of as her submissive one because I've seen no other like it, but the word doesn't truly describe it. Her eyes don't cloud with blind lust or willingness or even ecstasy when we reach that point. They're startling in their clarity, actually, because Red isn't lost in the moment. She's not lost in the emotions and sensations as so many would be, have been. She's completely with me—in the same frame of mind as me. Her lips will sometimes part for a small smile if I've allowed her the use of her mouth, and she'll breathe out one word, "more."

With Grace, though, it's all about control. I don't tie her up; I don't hurt her, well, much. I order her around. I don't push for her obedience; it's her eager willingness to comply that puts her into a pure state of submission where she aches to be whatever I want, whatever I need. There's no effort on my part required. I just enjoy the fruits of it. And then it's all me pushing for more.

I lightly pinch her left nipple, rolling the hardened pebble between my fingers and making her try not to squirm. I know that I won't have much for her, but I want to make her come. I love the small gasps and high-pitched squeals she tries to hold back when I get her there. So very different from the full-throat moans and screams I get from Red, but both are music to my ears.

"Open your legs. Wider." I kneel in between her thighs, looking down on her and no longer smiling. For whatever reason, Grace likes when I seem more angry than

happy with her during sex. She prefers the idea that her ability to please me is illusory in its quest. I learned this about her quickly. She comes harder for me when I add either humiliation or admonishment to sex. It's a game I'm willing to explore for her since the prize is her softness.

I decide to try to use her submissive state to get more out of her. My daily efforts for the last weeks to get information about her past have gotten me nowhere. Maybe open like this, she'll be more open to questions too. It's worth a shot.

"Grace, put your hands on the headboard." She does, pushing herself to me a little, legs spreading even wider. I suppress a smile at the anticipation on her face. I take her clit in between my fingers, and she gasps. It's still so swollen, only light pressure is needed to have her moaning and stiffening against the bed to stop moving.

"Did your Master before me make you moan like that?" I ask this quietly. I know she doesn't refer to the man who hurt her as Master. She doesn't like when I do either, but I want her a little uncomfortable right now. I hope that she finds this the right amount of humiliation. Bringing up her being with another like this is certainly enough of an image to add the required edge to my voice. I hold my breath waiting for her answer, watching her face frown as she wars the need to please me with the need to keep her secrets. She only shakes her head. "No. Answer me."

"No." It's a weak reply, held back with her breath.

"Did you like being under his control?" I'm feeling sick with my own questions and have to concentrate on her tits moving up and down with her quickened breaths, on the

feel of her slick lips as I slip a finger gently into her, in order not to lose my hard-on.

She shakes her head again, and I lightly slap her thigh to remind her to speak. "No." But I can see that I'm getting nowhere.

"Look at me, Grace. Tell me something, anything. Where did you live before, when you were with him?" I'm not faking the anger in my voice now. It's the frustration from weeks of trying to move the boulder that keeps her mouth shut against any details of her life before me.

She starts to shake her head but stops, and her eyes blank for just a moment. I keep my finger inside her, circling while I wait for the committee's decision. That's what it feels like—waiting to hear what all her selves will say, and even who will say it.

Her eyes fill with happiness, and she pushes into my finger more, but only what she can without moving too much still. Ever the obedient submissive that she is, she remembers my order to not move. I smile back, hopeful that this means I'm going to finally get some answers.

"We didn't live here. We did live with him. It was long ago and not like this, not like we are with you." That's it? That's all I'm going to get?! She closes her lips and pleads with her eyes, a fear creeping into them that I know well. She's afraid that she hasn't pleased me. I let go of my anger and smile more. I know she lived with him. That's something, I guess.

Yet knowing that another man had her—had Red, had any part of her—I'm not faking as my look hardens more, matching the hardness I place at her entrance. I decide to be cruel and give in to my inner demon that likes toying with her, likes taking her to the edge of her submission—her willingness to give up control so easily. I know another man had her willingness once, even as I know he was no match for me with Red. I don't care; jealousy is what drives me now.

I put my finger, the one still wearing her wetness, to her lips. "You won't make a sound. You won't move at all. And you won't come, Grace. You'll only feel me as I explode inside you." I watch her swallow and one tear escape down her cheek. But I know that even if I deny her a physical release, my warped game plays into her need to please. I've gotten used to dancing the line between my equal needs for cruelty and softness with Grace.

I close my eyes and push into her in one long, deep thrust. Her lips pull me, squeeze me, shudder around me, but I don't count this as disobedience. She's swollen from the hours I spent in her already. Even though she doesn't feel the pain, her poor pussy can't help but react to the pounding that I'm giving her now. Her arms and legs remain still; her face shows her concentration on not giving in to her own desires. Losing myself in watching her control—a control that I commanded—I only have a few deep, fast thrusts before I'm ready.

I fall onto her, pushed as far in as I can. My moans breathe in her hair, my body quivering her under me. "Come for me now, Grace. Give yourself to me, sweet girl." And it's all the permission she needs to gasp out the breath she was holding. Her arms and legs squeeze me, her lips tightening and releasing in quick, short convulsions in time with her squeaks. My need for her softness was greater than my need to be cruel tonight, I guess.

I drifted off to sleep that night imagining new ways to toy with her for her wicked secret keeping. I can almost smile now, thinking that I'll get a chance to use one of those ideas tonight. There's one that will work perfectly with the piano actually.

I don't dwell on those thoughts, not with Miles and Cary watching her. The lightning fast changes in her identities have become familiar to me, but I glance at them to see if they notice any difference in her. Both seem to just be enjoying her playing, following her delicate, long fingers as they fly across the keys.

Neither notices that her face has softened to an angelic wistfulness. Her eyes are half-closed, and her lips are wet and slightly parted. She appears to take up less of the seat, despite moving fluidly through the music. The dress that was provocative and sexy a moment ago, now seems too revealing for the shy, sweet woman filling the air with her haunting melody.

Seeing Grace here in place of Red only adds to the ill feeling in my stomach. I told her that my cousin wouldn't be the type of man I'd want her around, not until he understood how things were with us anyway. I had realized the irony but didn't share it with her. She obeyed just as she has the past weeks—without questioning. Too much at least. I knew Red could handle Cary. I wasn't so sure *I* could handle Red around him, but it was better than the alternative.

Watching as these two men admire her now is more jealousy than my newly possessive heart can take. I have to stop my second step towards her, still imagining the satisfaction I'd get from grabbing her arms and carrying her away from here caveman style—away from Miles Vanderson and even Cary.

But her music is calming. I allow it to have a soothing effect on me and can almost forget anyone else is in the room with us. The thought of her playing like this for me every night cools my anger enough that I can smile as she continues.

Grace always has this effect on me. Red can get my blood pumping faster than any woman I've ever known. Grace can soothe me with equal speed. What I feel for her, fuck, for *all* of her, it's insanity. Not for the first time today, I think I need to get my head straight—to get clear about what I want, what *she* needs, *us*.

Grace changes the score, cutting through the repeats and seguing to the end nicely. The silence fills the large room for only a moment; Cary breaks it with loud clapping and an impressed smile to me. I note that Miles doesn't clap, only grins at her. It bristles the hair on my neck, making me clench my jaw and fists again. He's giving Grace a fucking predatory smile.

I relax quickly as I walk over to her, hiding her from view with my back once more. I lift her chin, but her eyes aren't the softness I've come to crave from her. It's more of the fear I only glimpsed from Red. Her lips open; but she doesn't say anything, only shakes her head briefly and retreats again.

"That was beautiful, my dear." My fingers grip the piano edge hearing Miles address her this way again. Red stands and moves around me before I can stop her though.

The fear is still there, but she's countering it with her usual aggression. She's not frozen anymore at least.

"Thank you." Her husky voice is seductive, but I can hear the subtle shaking. I'm pleased to see that she doesn't step near him, though he gets an eyeful of her anyway. She stands tall for her petiteness—her usual confident stance that puts all her body on full display. Normally, I like it. Normally, it's just for me. Seeing her pose like this for another man makes my temples pulse. Fuck.

Cary seems to be enjoying his view too, but he lowers his eyes and turns away when he catches the menacing look on my face. Miles only smiles a little more, ignoring me still and speaking directly to Red, "Who taught you to play, Scarlet?" He stresses her name in an odd way, like a serpent hissing it.

She startles me by laughing. It's her usual deep, sensual laugh—the one I long to capture with my fingertips and lips each time. But she cuts it short. "Oh, it's a skill I picked up long ago. I've forgotten more than I care to remember." I raise an eyebrow to her. Red isn't flirting, but there's something in her tone that I'm missing. There's something in how she's standing and acting that is assertive even for her.

"I'm sure you could remember if you were encouraged, my dear." I don't need any more encouragement to kick this guy's ass, but he interrupts my turning around. "Are you attending the event tonight at Iron Horse?" I see Cary nod, and Miles turns to me. "Then perhaps we'll be able to discuss business more there." He nods to me once before walking quickly out of the room.

Anderson Valley: Red/Gigi

"Are you all right?" It's hard to distinguish Simon's words over the chaos in my head. He's being quiet too, keeping his voice low and near my ear. He obviously doesn't want his cousin to overhear him.

My eyes flutter from his hands on my arms to his eyes; I finally manage a smile. Simon's clear blue icicles crinkle in response, but I can see the worry etched on his strong features. His blond hair is more tousled from raking his fingers through it. My own fingers dance with a desire to reach up.

Simon's hot breath on my ear sends the familiar shiver to my spine. It crystalizes my thoughts, stabilizes my hold on my body. But the sensation is gone too quickly. Simon moves away, taking his heat with him.

From that first time meeting him, fucking him, I've wanted more. It's why I left his apartment so quickly. If I'd stayed, I would've begged him to tie me up and never let me leave his bed.

Now I wish I had. Instead, I listened to the others in my head, all saying I had to get away, all saying that it was a bad idea to get involved with yet another man. I don't count a few fleeting fuckscapades as getting involved, but I wasn't in a frame of mind to argue then.

I won't make the mistake of listening to them now though, not tonight.

I heard Grace explain "us" to Simon, that we're each a part and a whole by ourselves. I couldn't have said it better myself, except that I feel more separate, more whole, than the others. I've had more time to be me, Gigi, than they have. I'm able to cope with all of life's little challenges better than any of them. And I'll make my own decisions from now on, especially if they involve Simon. Or Miles.

The strained voices in the corner draw me back to the room, back to Simon. I try to concentrate on what he's saying to Cary. He's obviously mad. Cary is obviously trying to appease him. Neither man seems to know who Miles really is though. Good.

I feel a familiar ping in my head. The slapstick routine I secretly despise. It's *them*, the others I share this body with, the four that occupy too much of my time, and now, too much of Simon's. They're all clamoring to be heard, to be seen.

I no longer uphold the transparency of our mutual lives. I keep my time with Simon to myself, mostly. In part, it's to protect the little ones, but mostly it's to keep Grace at bay. She wants him for her own selfish reasons. But he chose me for tonight, and I'll be damned if I'm giving in to her demands, no matter what just happened.

Besides, I protected us once. I've earned the right to stay now. I'm the only one that can deal with Miles. They are all in a panic, but I can stay calm.

So what if the initial shock of seeing Miles here was enough to make me withdraw for a few minutes? I was shocked enough to leave the "stage" in our mind transparent. Grace, of course, jumped at the opportunity to show off for Simon. She took the limelight and played her boring music for him. A fleeting thought rolls my stomach. Was she really playing for Miles?

I knew she wouldn't stay long though. Grace is a coward. They all are. So I'm not about to give up the stage to her now, no matter how much pressure she tries to exert.

I force my focus back on to the here and now. It always helps to keep me grounded, present. I move my hands over our body, feeling the soft fabric of the dress I chose for Simon. Rubbing the smoothness of the silk on my back against the sting of the lash marks he left last night, I can heighten the feeling with a small twist of my shoulders.

I want to rip the dress off and demand he kiss the marks that he made. His lips always draw the perfect blend of cool relief tracing after his hot breath. Sometimes his teeth bring me further pain and claim a quick orgasm before I can even beg him for release. This is always met with more lashes for disobedience. A delicious shudder runs down my back with this thought.

Rubbing my finger over my lips, my hunger for him replaces all traces of fear. My perfect match. My sweet darkness. *My* Trust. *My* Simon.

There, that's better. The noise has stopped; I have the stage to myself, for now anyway. I can concentrate on what to do next.

Anderson Valley: Miles Vanderson

"Did you see her, Mr. Vanderson?" Spencer waited inside the car, out of sight along with his three associates. I didn't want it to seem as if I came here with an armed escort. I'm glad I chose to be low-profile, for now at least.

"Yes. Gillian will be at the event tonight. We'll be able to take her there."

Spencer nods, checking his .45 Sar K2 automatic and returning it to a concealed holster. Now that his investigation is complete, I've kept him on as head of a private team to ensure Gillian's safe return to my home. He's proved himself invaluable thus far and will be just as tenacious in guarding my Gillian as he was in tracking her down.

After Gillian disappeared in San Francisco, he wasted no time in finding her again. The connection with Simon Lamb was tenuous though. Spencer couldn't confirm if she was with him of her own volition or as one of his abducted trainees. Her disappearance had been abrupt after meeting Simon and with very little clues either way.

Just the thought of her with another man was enough to push me into a homicidal rage. Knowing that man could have held her with the intent to train her as a sex slave for sale drove me beyond any impulse to anger I'd ever known before.

I warned Spencer that I would hold him personally responsible for her safe return to me, but the welfare of anyone else involved was not his concern. The man may not be educated, but he certainly didn't miss my meaning. He's the perfect man for this job. Money is the only language that he speaks.

His bloodhound skills came in handy uncovering everything there is to know about Simon Lamb too, although there weren't a lot of details to be found. I know now that Simon's family is moneyed. His mother died with his birth; his father died when he was very young. He was raised by a doddering old grandfather who overindulged and allowed him to get into all sorts of trouble. Lamb seemed to get himself under control quickly, though, because tales about his antics ended by the time he reached his junior year in a private college prep school. His grandfather died shortly after, and he became sole heir to the family wealth.

I also learned that Lamb values his privacy almost as much as I do.

Finding a contact, a way to get closer to him, was still easy. A few shrewdly placed inquiries was all it took to get the proper introductions. Cary Lamb isn't as cautious as his cousin.

"I'll have the jet ready to leave tonight, Sir." Spencer is already on his phone. I only nod and turn to watch the passing of hills with gnarled grape vines silhouetted against the darkening sky.

But it's not the wine country that I see. It's *her*.

Spencer wanted to make the introductions, thinking it prudent to keep my identity secret. I needed to see her with my own eyes though. It's been three long years since I've seen Gillian. She was exactly as I remember her. Slight and slim, her body was deceptively curved with how she stood. Her bones jutted out appealingly, hips begging to be grasped. Her hair, a wild mane of chestnut, fell down her back and sprang up all around her in a natural halo, just as I recall from memory. Her soft, full lips were a shade too dark against her pale creaminess tonight.

And her eyes, it's her eyes I remember most: how they would dart around in fear, how they would relax and widen in perfect submission, how the deep chocolate brown was made darker with her emotions. Always so readable, always so expressive, Gillian's eyes gave everything away so easily even in her blankest looks. Tonight was no different.

I knew she wasn't my Gillian when I walked in. I could tell by the way she stood, the set of her lips, and the coolness to her eyes. She quickly changed for me. The flash flickering between her selves happened before either Lamb could see it, I'm sure.

When she obeyed my command to play the piano, I knew neither man saw the change in her. Neither man saw the *real* Gillian. *My* sweet Gillian.

Neither could see how her eyes softened, her head bowed. Neither could truly appreciate how beautifully she danced her fingers across the keys, so light and pleasing. Neither knew she learned to play just to please me.

"I've hired an excellent instructor to teach you classical piano. She'll come here daily for your lessons starting this afternoon." In the darkened bedroom, curtains drawn, I pick up Gillian's hand from her bare lap. *"Your fingers are too fine to not be used to their full potential."* I kiss the tip of each digit before pulling her palm up to kiss the fleshy base of her thumb, giving it a bite.

She only blinks her submission to my demand. Of course she wouldn't argue.

"Do you really think anyone can teach her? She's a little old to start lessons now." Her mother's voice is harsh as usual. *I'd prefer to ignore Anya altogether but know this isn't an option.*

Putting Gillian's hand gently back down onto her lap, I cup her face with my fingers, squeezing her cheeks against her teeth. Her eyes narrow for a moment against the discomfort. "She's still young, only 15." I know this will upset Anya, a reminder of youth she'll never possess again. "She'll learn. She has no choice. I'll beat her for every wrong note." Gillian barely flinches at this announcement. I know Anya will enjoy adding to the list of reasons to discipline her daughter. Without turning, I can hear the smile in her response.

"You have more faith in her than I do, sweet boy." I don't like her endearment; it's meant to be a reminder of my lowly status as fledgling heir.

But I know how to get Anya off her high horse quickly. "Have you been to the doctor as Father demanded?" Her response is nothing more than a snorted chuckle, and I can hear the underlying frustration. The picture of a horse is accurate. She's bridling with the desire to tell her husband just what he can do with his demands. Letting Gillian's face go, I turn around. "Not to worry. I'm sure you'll have a clean bill of health again this year, sweet Stepmother."

I've certainly paid enough to make sure the doctors stay quiet about Anya's inability to conceive, but I haven't told her that. If Anya were to go, Gillian would go as well. I can't allow that. Still, I won't grant Anya the satisfaction of thinking that we're partners in her deceptions either. Keeping Father tied to a sterile wife ensures my status as heir remains unquestioned. It's a win-win for me. I won't have Gillian's mother thinking she has the upper hand with any of this though.

"I can only hope to keep up with your father's virulence. He's a man that certainly knows how to keep a woman satisfied." Yet another of her cheap jibes.

I laugh at her words since her fingers unconsciously dip into the fold below her hairy mound, still glistening with sweat and fluids from the last hour of our being together.

I'm confident my frail and failing father is no match for my prowess in satisfying his much younger wife. And he certainly doesn't know her penchant for including her teenage daughter in her depravity. As witness or participant, it's now entirely up to me what role she plays, and I much prefer Gillian as participant. I can keep myself harder longer with her involvement.

"Gillian, I believe your mother is in need of a good tongue lashing for her insolence." Anya and I are in complete agreement that her daughter should be kept busy thinking of ways to please and submit. I don't mind sharing the fruits of these thoughts with her mother. Of course I would prefer to have Gillian all to myself, but for now, I must be respectful of the woman that created my sweet girl in the first place.

A bump in the winding road brings my attention back to the current night and the excitement of finally finding Gillian again. Watching her play for me just now, I realize that no matter what else took place over the last three years of her disappearance, she's still mine. My rage isn't subdued, but I can wait until we're alone to indulge in venting it. I can hold on to this false civility a little longer. She's been hiding behind the whore façade for three years, but for me, she'll return to her *true* self. *My* obedient Gillian.

And she'll pay for her betrayal. She has three years to atone for, starting tonight.

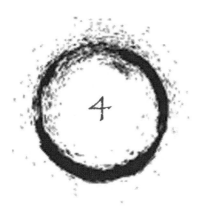

Anderson Valley: Red/Gigi

Turning to the corner, focusing on Simon, a smile plays across my lips despite all the stress of seeing Miles again. Simon will protect me, us. Look at how furious he is with his cousin just for bringing a stranger here. He doesn't even know the truth about Miles, but he instinctively didn't like him, obviously.

Simon's back and shoulders tense under his suit jacket, only accentuating his raw masculinity. His light blond hair and blue eyes add to his sweet good looks, at odds with the steel in his voice and the darkness that I know lurks under every stretch of his sculpted muscles. I lick my lips at the thought of his body against mine.

I've never met a man like Simon. He's flawed but beautiful, strong, all-consuming and possessive. He fills my head with desires so precisely, so exquisitely. His sensual mouth is only the start of my unraveling. I could spend hours exploring his desires.

Most surprisingly, I have yet to reach any limits with him, though I know he'll take me further down to deeper fathoms. Either that or I'll push him there myself. I arch an eyebrow at this pleasant thought.

The others don't understand this; they don't understand him. Grace thinks she does, but only *we* understand each other. I see inside Simon, into every corner of *his* stage. He doesn't fully embrace the darker parts of himself; most times, he holds back and thinks through his next move, weighs his desires against what is demanded of him. Only when he's unleashing those desires on me is he fully the man he's meant to be. Maybe he was like this when he was training a product too? But I prefer not to think about that, just like I prefer to ignore his time with Grace. I know what *we* have together.

Simon, my Trust, understands my desire to be completely open to the blackness inside; it mirrors his own needs. We don't shy away from the exposed and unhealed within us that the others so protectively hide from. I haven't told him any secrets, but he instinctively reacts when I rip open the curtains and reveal a dark corner in my mind. He pushes me to give him my pain, the old and new, consuming it all and making it his own.

The others don't understand pain. They don't get what it can be, what it can do. With the lash of a whip, I tear through the memories we five share and the darkest memories I keep to myself. I merge the feel of a new mark with ones I've worn in our past. I amplify the pain with the memories, adding fire to the fever of every sexual encounter, even the most vanilla.

It's how we survived, how I thrived.

With Trust, I've reveled in those memories more than ever before. I've searched them all out, bringing them to the surface to give him my pain. I've taken strength in what they are, a beacon calling him deeper.

He doesn't back away from the darkness; he wades into the murkiest shadows with me. We share a need that blends everything into one long grasp for the improbable. It's a healing to a tear, a filling of a void, a bending to a demand for more. And I give it all to him, laying open every remembered tear, every void, every demand to make it his own, *our* own.

He's given me this strength to bow to his need. It is freely offered, and he wants nothing in return but my acceptance of his desire to have it all.

And I've succumbed to the absolute power of the man that pulls, culls, calls my unwitting submission. I've embraced the power of that submission to draw him in further, to have him kneeling and worshipping what he's conquered. I've known surrender and strength with him, true freedom, and a hell of a lot of orgasms.

I won't call it love. I won't degrade what we have with such a small word.

Love is what I had for Miles. Love is what made me his fool before. I'm not a fool with Simon; I'm his match. That's so much more than love could ever be. It's perfection at its ugliest darkness, and I've never been happier.

I won't give it up. I won't let Miles take this from me, no matter what he's planning with showing up here tonight.

For all my years of freedom, even my weeks with Simon, I haven't realized until this moment all that I've gained from both. A quiet strength. A deeper understanding of myself. My selves.

Our existences have always been troubled. It's not an easy thing for me to admit though, even to myself, that I haven't always felt secure. I've always had a clear understanding of my place on the stage among the others, but out in the world among people who are unchanging, I've been uncertain of my fit.

The pain of those insecurities is one that I won't be reliving or remembering. I'm through with doubts.

I know I have it easier than any of the others with this. I knew my place as the bearer of Mother's sickness, letting most of it wash over me without allowing it to carve a place in my heart. I took what she did. I took the pain and made it my own.

I took what Miles did as well. For a while, I even called that love. But I won't give up what I have now for him.

Simon will help me. He'll help us.

Anderson Valley: Simon Lamb

"Never again, Cary." I've kept my voice low. If I raise it, I'll let more of my anger out than I want. I'll not be able to contain the urge to pummel my cousin. He's responded appropriately, apologizing and acquiescing, but I still want to throttle him for bringing a stranger here—an arrogant fucking stranger who rattled Red, who dared to touch her. Fuck.

I turn as Red saunters slowly over to us. "Are you two done squabbling? I'm famished." She appears to be back to normal. Whatever spell of fear she was under is gone completely. Her smile is teasing and helps to relax the last of my anger.

I give her a grin back and grab her around the waist to pull her in for a kiss. As always, Red anticipates my every move. Her head tilts back, lips part, eyelids lower, but her eyes challenge me to take her mouth roughly. In response, my lips just whisper over hers; my tongue only darts teasingly across her lips. She slides a hand up my chest and around my neck in an attempt to pull me in for more; but she stops with the slightest shake of my head, our lips barely brushing. Her hand turns to a fist in my hair, tugging slightly, but she obediently remains at my control. Her lips only part more. I know she likes the anticipation as much as I do.

I can hear Cary moving away, and it breaks the spell. I turn my lips to her cheek and bury my nose in her hair, taking a deep breath in of her spicy sweetness. I'll have to adjust the press against my zipper before we leave.

Red runs her hands over the sides of her dress, lips twitching with a secret smile at the knowledge of what she does to me. I watch her take Cary's arm. She leads him towards the foyer, and I have to stifle the impulse to grab her away from him.

I'm not pleased with the prospect of seeing Miles again tonight, but it will give me a chance to set him straight on a few things. Red's deep laugh trails ahead of me out the door.

I'll get a few things straight with her too when we're home tonight—her and Grace and the rest. Fuck. Shaking my head as the door is closed behind me, I must be as insane as she is.

Anderson Valley: Simon Lamb

The promise of what's to come—that's summertime in wine country. It's a heady anticipation of what science, devotion and hard labor can birth in a few short months. It's also the perfect time to celebrate seasons passed.

Events in the valleys are numerous and usually avoidable for me, but Iron Horse was one of Grandfather's favorites. He never missed a tasting if he was in town. An original bottle of sparkling wine still holds a place of honor amongst our racks of chilled champagnes.

My being here tonight is out of respect for him. It was something he said in the letter he left for me—a part of his legacy, his wish that I become the man he saw in me.

Despite letting our own lands lapse, Grandfather was a devoted follower to estate winemakers. He admired the will it takes to cultivate raw earth into liquid dreams. He pressed me to be inspired by the blend of romance and backbone. This is one of my concessions to his dying wishes. That and the wine is exceptional.

It will hopefully help take the edge off my nerves tonight. After Red's frozen state earlier, I was hesitant to bring her out in public. She laughed and flirted more than I liked during the ride here, but she also avoided my eyes. She didn't blank or pull away, but something about her demeanor remained aloof and withdrawn. Each time I questioned her with my glances, she turned away.

With my hand firmly on her lower back, leading us towards a group of small tables, I smile to myself. Shackled and flogged, I'll get my answers from her tonight.

"Have you been to a barrel tasting before, Scarlet?" I cringe hearing that stupid name. Between Grace and Red, I already have a hard time keeping things straight. Now I have to contend with yet another name in the mix, and it's my own fault. I quietly growl at my cousin; he hasn't left her side. He keeps brushing his shoulder and arm against her.

"No. Although something tells me, Cary, that you'll make an excellent instructor for a virgin." He laughs and makes a promise to teach her everything he knows. My cousin may have capitulated to my anger earlier, but he's also a smartass and doesn't take being reprimanded easily, even by me. He's only smiled sarcastically at me each time I give him a warning look to back off. Fucker has a death wish tonight.

Red gives me her best innocent smile and latches her arm around Cary's. "We'll be right back, Simon." Before I can grab her arm without looking ridiculous, she pulls him away. I grab the top of a chair and grip it with the force I'd like to apply to her throat instead. She's been wickedly enjoying pushing my buttons on purpose tonight.

Distracted watching her move among the crowd with Cary, I only become aware of the man to my right when I turn slightly. Miles is watching Red too, but his look is neutral. He turns with me and smiles at my hand on the chair. I release my hold and turn to face him fully. Good, someone I can vent a little of this hostility towards.

"She's a lovely creature. A walking advertisement for your training?" Miles appears amused by the anger still plain on my face.

"*She's* none of your business." I say this low and quiet to not attract any attention, but there can be no mistaking the edge to my voice.

Miles feigns ignorance to its meaning though. "Oh. That's too bad. I was interested in acquiring her. She's *almost* perfectly what I want, Mr. Lamb." He's lucky that he didn't add a lascivious look in her direction, or I'd be walking out of here with a hit to my reputation and raw knuckles.

Before I can comment though, he leans in, taking more personal space than I care to share. "Of course, if you change your mind, I could make it worth your while. Money means nothing to me when it comes to getting what I want."

I resist the desire to take a step away from his cologne. Barely keeping the rising anger from my voice, I speak clearly, "As I already said, *Miles,* I'm not the man for the job. And *she's* not the woman either." He again appears to size me up in some way. His eyebrows raise and lower quickly, as though he's forming some assessment of me I don't care to know about.

Taking a split second to calm my mounting rage, I'm able to meet his eyes with a little mirth and continue more in control before he can interrupt. "I'm sure Bradford explained that this is a business that requires discretion. I don't think knocking on my door meets that criteria. Where did you say you met him?"

His smile twitches and eyes narrow minutely, but I get a better impression of the man in that brief moment. He's not just uncomfortable; he's fighting to maintain control of himself. Probably one of those men who thinks having a woman under his thumb would be the ultimate testament to just how much of a fucking man he is.

It takes a lot more than money to hold the reins over any woman. A man like this one would never understand that. Even if I wasn't too distracted with Red right now, I wouldn't let Miles anywhere near one of my products. He doesn't strike me as the type to appreciate the amount of finesse it takes to turn a woman into a willing slave.

His brief break in a calm exterior over, Miles delivers his response smoothly enough. "I didn't, and I don't think it would be discreet to discuss that any further here." His palm indicates the people milling about close by.

It's the only thing I agree with him about so far. Still, I'm not willing to let him off the hook that easily. "I've not seen you in Bradford's social circle before. Are you new to the Bay area?"

"I am, but I have family here." He looks over the room, like he's searching for someone. I glance around too but no longer see Cary or Red. "I won't be staying long though." He turns to look me up and down once more, narrowing his eyes in disdain. "Unlike you, Mr. Lamb, I'm not retired. I have certain *obligations* that must be respected."

His superior bullshit is spiking my anger again, but I manage to keep my voice even. "You should look for a new market for your product needs, Miles. I don't think San Francisco is going to pan out for you. Enjoy your evening." I walk away without another look at his smirking face.

That did a little to cool my wrath, but I have a gnawing pit in my stomach still as I find Cary and Red, laughing in a circle of men. Clearly, she's been her usual entertaining self. Her eyes sparkle when she turns to the slight pinch I give her back, right on a spot I know bears my mark. The corners of her mouth raise in a delicious smile. I can't resist kissing each corner and running my tongue across her velvety lips.

Her eyes flick briefly behind me before turning back towards Cary. Her back is a little stiffer, her voice a little higher than normal as she continues talking with him. I follow where her gaze went and grind my teeth at a nod from Miles. He turns quickly away though, and I lose sight of him in the crowd.

Anderson Valley: Red/Gigi

I can feel his eyes on me. Having Simon and Cary close only alleviates the tension slightly. I knew coming here tonight would lead to confrontation. I only hope that Miles will continue to be on his best behavior. He obviously doesn't want to alarm Simon or reveal himself in any way. Neither do I, not until I have a plan in place.

One thing's for sure; I may not know what Miles is up to, but I know he won't leave until he's had his say. The bastard always had to have the last word. I'm not a naïve 17 year old girl anymore though. Whatever game he's playing, he won't win. Not this time. Not if I can help it.

The others are all silent, waiting for the implosion they're expecting. I may have been thrown off, seeing Miles out of the blue after all this time, but I won't be afraid of him. I won't, dammit. I refuse to let him make any of us afraid anymore.

The quiet in my head is unsettling. I've never known this level of isolation. Having the stage to myself is one thing, but this feeling of loneliness is all new. My ears throb with my heartbeat. My throat isn't able to stop swallowing, needing to get the lump down that just won't budge, and my damn knees keep locking.

I know it's fear. I can withdraw from pain, take from it what I like. Fear is another animal. I have no control over it. I've had to endure more than my share of it to protect the others; it appears tonight will be no different.

Simon's hand is gentle on my back and side but ever present. He seems intent on staking his claim with his overbearing physique. He's pulled and pushed me away from any contact with other men in the area. That's fine by me. I'm having a hard time keeping up with the surrounding chatter. My eyes keep dragging through the crowd, searching for a face I'd hoped to never see again.

Grace was technically the last to see Miles, but we all watched when he hurt her. It was three years ago, and the memory of that night is as vivid as any of my own. Lost in the security of Simon's embrace, I can't stop myself from feeling everything again from that last night with Miles, everything Grace felt.

"Gillian, I've spoken to your doctors today." Grace
sits on his bed with her hands laced loosely behind her back,
as he likes, and her eyes lowered to his lips, as she likes.
From my spot on the stage, I'm close but not quite touching
her; the others are further back in the shadows. I can feel
her excitement at being near him with the door closed. I
know I'll be in her place soon by the look on his face though.
Menacing is the word that bounces in my thoughts.
Whatever he wishes to say will be spoken with his whip as
much as his voice tonight. I feel a shudder of anticipation.

"They told me that you've made great progress." Miles
pats her head, and Grace eats up his approval. "They said
they've given you tools for fixing yourself." I feel a new
tension. It's my own, electric in its intensity, but I feel only
excitement from Grace still. She leans into his hand, now
cradling her head. "But they also said you've refused to use
these tools to their full potential, my love."

A spike in my anxiety hits, and I almost push Grace out
of the way. I hold off a little longer though. Miles has
steadily demanded more time with her ever since he
introduced us to the doctors last year. And even though I no
longer hold a place in my heart for him, because I know he
doesn't have a place for me in his, fool that he is, I still like
the freedom of being out. I enjoy his brand of painful love all
the same. I don't care if he pretends that I'm her, so long as
I get what I need from him. I wait now to exchange places
until the last minute though. Unlike when Mother was doling
out the punishments, I know it's Grace he wants.

I no longer care that he loves her or that she loves him still. Their love is meaningless to me as long as I get what I want in the end. And I have my plan for that.

Miles moves his hand from open to fisting her hair, but I continue to hold off because he keeps talking in his calm and distinct way with only a little pull to her head to bring her eyes up to his. "I've let the doctors go, Gilli." A thrill of delight from all of us at this good news is quickly thwarted as he continues, "You won't be needing their help anymore, my love. I will help you to be whole."

Grace doesn't need a push from us to ask what we all want to know. "What are you going to do, Miles?"

Not the way I would've phrased it, but I wait to breathe until he answers, "Come with me, Gilli. I'll show you."

She brings her hands around, and he grips both her wrists in one of his hands, leading her quickly out the door. Walking this way, with her arms as a leash, I can feel Grace suffering with the yank to her shoulders. Still, I wait to exchange places. Something in how calm Miles is behaving makes me hesitate. I think he'll reveal more to Grace than me. I always seem to push his more sadistic tendencies a little quicker than she does.

I smile to myself, hiding it from Lilly, who is watching me from her darker corner of the stage. I don't mind his violence, but I think it's important to see his reasoning for getting rid of the doctors. Grace will get that answer faster than I can.

Finally, Miles stops in front of a door, down a long, nearly empty corridor. It's not so much a door as it is a panel to the wall in a part of the mansion that goes unused.

Servants keep this area looking as spotless as any other, but I've only ever been here once before. Lilly tried to lock herself in one of the rooms when Mother first married Martin, foolishly thinking she could wait out one of Mother's bad tempers in hiding. I knew better.

The panel of wood that resembles a door glides effortlessly open and reveals a black expanse of unknown size behind it. I didn't see how he opened it, but it's obvious as he yanks Grace through the doorway that he has a remote for it somewhere. It shuts automatically behind her. When the door is fully closed without so much as a sound or gush of air, a light above her head flicks on, providing a sickly yellow glow but doing nothing to reveal the space still. Their footfalls echo as Miles leads her farther in.

I can feel her heart pounding, smell the cool mustiness, but I can't see beyond Miles' back and the darkness around her in their slow procession. After a few feet, another yellow light turns on, illuminating again only a small circle of the same cool gloom. Their progress continues another few feet until a final light goes on at a dead end.

Miles' voice cuts the shadowy silence, causing Grace to jump. "This house was used as a warehouse and speakeasy in the Prohibition era. My family ran liquor through here from Canada. This hallway we're in now was part of their escape tunnel. It was connected with other tunnels and rooms before my father converted it into a safe room."

The dead end turns out to be another door, gliding as soundlessly open as the first. Miles grins as he pulls Grace through the opening. The sound of the click echoes when it shuts behind them. Another yellow light reveals a tiny cell of a room.

He finally lets go of Grace's hands, and she turns to face him. "Father did all the work himself. He made sure that the secret tunnels, and especially this room, remained a secret. They were never on any plans or drawings of the house, even during the many renovations over the years."

Miles moves closer, putting his hands around Grace's waist and pressing her chest to his stomach. I can feel how her head warms with his lips pressed to her hair. "So you see, Gilli? In this room, it's just you and me, and no one else knows we're here, my love."

I feel a cold shudder make its way up my back, reminding me of bugs with many legs. I've never been afraid of bugs though. Little things like that can be crushed so easily. But this room is too familiar, too similar. I feel the air turning hot in Grace's lungs and realize she's held her breath and risks fainting.

I take her place, brushing her aside easily. I can't let us pass out in here with Miles, not like this.

Taking in one deep breath of the stale air and steadying myself against the familiar feel of being closed in, I feel Miles tense against me. He knows the change now as it happens. Over the last two years, he's become very familiar with all the subtleties of our personality shifts.

He pulls back and looks into my eyes, and I look into his. I'm frightened. He's not as I expected, not angered by my being here. The sweet look he reserves for only Grace is absent as well; it's a false front for what he harbors in his heart, but he still keeps the pretense of sweetness with her *usually. This is different. He's not looking through me and seeing what he wants to see. Her. He's looking right at me, seeing me like he did when he broke my heart a year ago.*

Grace may have been the last to see him, but I was the one who woke up the next day, relieved to find that I was alone in my bed. Miles had left for work as usual, like everything was normal. Poor Grace was curled in a ball in the darkest corner of the stage, not even crying, just whimpering. She stayed like that for a long time too, even when I told her we were safe and away from him.

Miles had locked the bedroom door, probably told the staff that I wasn't to be disturbed all day. He'd done that before, locked us away with no food, no care. It was perfect for me, perfect for my plan. I wasn't going to wait around for him to return.

The night before, when the stage shook with Grace's screams, I knew I'd have to follow through with my plan. It was a plan I kept to myself while I held the littlest ones, Baby and Lilly. Jill wouldn't join us but stayed close in the corner, covering her ears during the loudest screams.

The doctors Miles made us visit said we should try to merge our existences and memories into one identity. They were convinced we could be whole again and healed if we embraced all five memories as one. All bullshit. We all shared that memory of Miles torturing Grace that night, each in our own way. We didn't leave her alone, but we were helpless to save her.

I wasn't helpless that next morning though. I acted quickly. I remember how the sheet stuck to my back from crusts of blood dried overnight. I didn't wince as I tore it free. I was used to that treatment from him, although he usually didn't break the skin. It wasn't the same pain like I now relish with Simon, but I could take it.

I washed the wounds the bastard made and smiled that he'd left my face alone as usual. Miles had learned from Mother that beatings should remain hidden. It worked in my favor that day. I got us away. I got us enough money to hide and live free from him.

The years before became a blur, a white hot steam that fueled me and blinded me to anything except my will to escape. That last year with just Miles as our guardian was the hardest in a long line of hard years, but I didn't linger on those memories.

Miles pushed us to be what he wanted, what we'd never succeed in becoming. Without the threat from my mother or his father, Miles was free to let his more sadistic side out, but he was never as cruel as he was that last night, at least not with Grace.

We had to get away, and I had to be the one to do it. I used all of the pain and fear I'd felt over the last two years with Miles to fuel my escape from him. I didn't let the others know my plan until it was too late to stop me. On the bus ride to Sacramento, I explained it to them. I explained how we'd each have our time on the stage, how no one would ever tell us what to do again, and how we'd take care of each other. We'd be okay. No one would hurt us. No one would ever lock us in a lonely room again.

I didn't show the anxiety I felt at being alone, away from everything we'd ever known. I knew we all harbored that same fear. I didn't show the panic I felt at what would happen if Miles found us either.

That was before we met Simon. We never imagined meeting someone like him, someone who could accept us as we are. His arm is loose around my waist, but I lean in so I can feel his warmth more. Simon smiles down on me, both of us lost in each other before his attention is given back to Cary.

I haven't told him anything. We all agree that sharing our past is off limits, even with Simon. He's been surprisingly accepting of this too.

He treats each of us as individuals. As much as it pains me to think, I'm sure he's become fond of each of us in our own ways too, although he doesn't know our names. We've never told anyone, not even Mother, our names, but Simon has gotten to know all of us.

Baby secretly calls him Daddy. He buys her licorice and art supplies. He frames the pictures she makes for him and even displays them proudly in his room and the hallways. No one has ever done this for her before. Each morning, he has breakfast with her in private. We've smiled watching them. Her laughter threatens to crack the glass ceiling of the sunroom some mornings, but Simon always smiles and laughs with her.

Lilly takes extra time in preparing readings for him each day. She wants to impress him with her knowledge of the signs and planets. No one since Martin has given her such individualized attention. She's always been too shy to read her horoscopes out loud for anyone, even Martin; usually Grace would do it for her. With Simon, Lilly has insisted on reading them herself. He's been indulgent and thoughtful, but he never presses for information about our past or how she knows all that she does about astrology.

Jill has been the biggest surprise. She normally doesn't want the stage at all, unless it's to react to her tormented, pent-up anger. She doesn't come out often around people. Every once in a while, she'll ask if she can sit with Simon, usually just a few minutes at a time and only when there's a game or movie on that she likes. We've all been impressed with his calming effect on her. Except for the beheading of the roses, she hasn't exploded with her usual rage since that first night with Simon.

And of course, Grace is in love with him. She won't admit it, but it's obvious with her soft, mooning stares. She keeps the stage transparent mostly, but I've refused to watch him with her. She can have the softer side of Simon because I know what he really wants. Me.

My plan had worked. We were away from Miles and safe. With Simon, we each even have a little hope and happiness.

But now Miles is here, and I'm as alone as I was that day after he hurt Grace three years ago. The others are too paralyzed with fear to do anything but cower and wait. I'm afraid too, but I don't have the luxury of hiding, and I'm not good at waiting.

"I'll be right back." I pat Simon's hand that is already squeezing harder around my arm.

Anderson Valley: Simon Lamb

"Where are you going?" I pull Red closer to my side, not letting her leave. Cary arches a brow but doesn't turn his head to us more. I know I should keep my voice down. I've already acted like a crazy asshole tonight, pushing Red around and keeping myself between her and anyone else.

Something feels off though, and I'm on edge. Red keeps nervously looking around, her head like a fucking bird's pivoting all over. It's not like her. Her laugh is even off.

"I'm just going to the bathroom." Her voice is still too high-pitched. Red pats my hand again, but she won't meet my eyes. I'm tempted to demand that Grace talk to me. I think I could get a straight answer out of *her* since she responds better to my domineering ways. The only thought that stops me is a memory of the coldness that invaded Red's look the last time I asked to talk to Grace instead of her. I can't do that to her again.

I'm struck once more by the insanity of my own thoughts and how easily I've gotten used to all of this.

I've had my share of women. Hell, I've had my share of sharing women. I've even had up to four women in bed with me at one time. It gets complicated and interesting real fast. But I've never had anything like I do with Red or Grace, or any of the others that I just call "Grace" because I don't know what else to call them.

There it is again—*them.* I'm in over my head with how complicated and interesting it's gotten.

Grace is the answer to everything submissive that I've ever wanted. I've not set out to train a girl to be mine before, but if I had, it'd be Grace. But Red is the answer to everything that I've never known I wanted. Fuck.

Okay. To myself, I can admit it. I like them both equally. *Like*? What am I, 15? Okay, *more* than like, I *want* them both. I *have* them both. So why does everything feel lopsided tonight? Like I'm the only one in the room that can feel the ground shaking with a 9.0 quake?

I take a deep breath and twist our bodies around so my back is to the small group of men that Cary is talking with still. I lean over her and can't keep the growl out of my voice as hard as I try. "I don't know what's going on with you tonight, Red, but you're going to tell me when we get home." She only blinks up at me. "Fine. You have five minutes, then we're leaving." She pulls away, but I snap her back to my side once more. "And stay the hell away from the man that came to my house earlier." She only nods, so I squeeze her to me harder. "I mean it, Red." She looks up at me, and I wish I could tell what she's thinking. She's not blank, not withdrawn, but she might as well be. She only nods again. Fuck.

I finally let her go and watch as she moves back to the edge of the room. I lose her to the crowd. I felt this way when she didn't show up in Chinatown or Castro last year. I'd lost control when I lost her. It's not a familiar feeling for me and definitely not one I'd welcome ever again.

Grace has been beyond unusual for me in so many ways. Embracing her dissociative identity disorder, well, it's been a crazy ride, even beyond what I expected last year when I followed her. Fuck, then she was just a quiet, shy girl I meant to take and train. It seems like years ago but was only four weeks yesterday when I brought her to my home with the intention of keeping her as my personal slave. That means four weeks of being lost in my obsession for everything about her.

In one night, I went from a man in complete control over everything in my life to a mixed-up mess, falling for a chick way more fucked up than I ever could have imagined. Falling for her? Fuck, try already *fallen*, jackass.

And now? Now I feel completely out of control again. This was a bad idea, bringing her out in public like this. I don't want to expose her to anyone. I don't want to *share* her

with anyone, not even a room full of innocuous strangers.
She might think me crazy with my obsession, but takes one
to know one, sweetheart. A half smile cracks through the
strain of my pressed lips.

"You all right, man?" Cary's voice cuts into my
thoughts. I nod, and he moves slightly away again but not
far. He's keeping an eye on me.

Cary has always had the ability to see through me. He's
always been able to react to my subtle mood shifts. I like to
think that I'm mysterious and can hold my shit together
pretty well, but I'm an open book to him and his sister,
Sophia. And now Grace and Red can read me too. Guess the
only mystery is how long I'm going to hold on to a false
image of myself. That has me smiling slightly again.

I try to relax more and return to the conversation, but I
can feel every muscle twitching. I down my glass of
remaining pinot and make this an excuse to leave the group
behind. My way towards the back, where the restrooms are,
is hindered by non-stop attempts to pull me into other small
circles though—women I've fucked; women who want to
fuck me; men I've known, some as clients; men who want to
get to know me, some as clients; and a few of Grandfather's
friends. For those, I stop briefly.

Closer to the back, I finally have a clear view of Red,
and she's doing exactly what I told her not to do—
purposefully trying to drive me up a fucking wall again by
talking to Miles. He has his hand on her waist and a shit
eating grin. I can't see her face, but the look on his says he
likes whatever he's hearing.

I take a big step towards her and knock right into a waiter clearing a tray of glasses off a table. In the shattering noise and flying glass shards, I take my eyes off Red.

When I look back up, she's alone and looking right at me. For a moment, I could swear she's Grace again, but my own anger, the distance and distractions make it hard to tell.

She doesn't move, so I make my way to her.

Anderson Valley: Red/Gigi

It didn't take long for Miles to spot that I was alone. I watch out of the corner of my eye as he beelines for me.

I turn and smile at him last minute, so he comes to a quick halt, his hand still reaching out to me. I brace myself for the collision of his flesh with mine, but Miles withdraws his hand like he can feel the heat rolling off me. I certainly feel my skin flushing with anticipation.

"Miles Vanderson." I don't enjoy saying his name, but I do like the way a crease forms between his brows at my confidence. "*You're* a long way from home."

"It seems I had to travel a great distance and invest a good amount of time to get back what's *mine*." He's not looking around or even nervous. I've been standing so still and tense that I can no longer feel my toes. I glance once around the crowd, wary of taking my eyes off him. Could some of these men be working for him?

"Looks like you traveled all this way for nothing then." I give myself points for not showing the nerves currently fraying my will to stand up to him.

"Not at all, my dear. I can see my prize clearly, and I *know* I won't be leaving here empty-handed." He's too confident. I search his face for a sign of what he has planned, a hint of how far he's willing to go in public like this. Appearances were always so important to him. I get nothing more than a broadened smile and a tilt of his head. It's the composed and intimidating look he inherited from his father, without any of the kindness.

I've seen a few women glance our way, longing to take my place and talk with the handsome stranger. He's good at fooling people into only seeing what he wants. We're alike in that regard. The cold and calculating side of him can stay hidden or be brought out whenever he likes. The evil that emanates from him remains in the shadows. He always concealed it, except when he had us alone.

I can't stop the shudder that rolls up my back and forces my shoulders to tilt forward. The memory of that last encounter with him still commands my thoughts.

Miles drops his hands from my waist and takes one step back, looking me up and down slowly. "I thought this might be too much for her to take." His lips quirk with a malicious smile, holding in a merciless laugh. His voice thuds against the cold, close walls of this hidden room.

I can feel the surfaces wanting to crush me; the tightness of the space threatens to stop my breathing. I can push this away though. I've done it before, and I can do it now. Just breathe, dammit! Slow and steady, that's it.

I stand a little taller, bracing myself for his cruelty as I always do. I'm able to meet his stare when his eyes return to mine. There's no softness, no sweetness, just that cruel narrowing that usually comes before his first strike. Even though he continues to see me, his words are aimed at Grace; he speaks right through me, as though I'm inconsequential to him. That's a blow that hurts my pride and heart, but I take it like any other, without flinching.

"The doctors were unsuccessful in convincing you to be whole again, Gilli, but I think this room will have the desired effect." His eyes circle around the enclosure before landing on me again. "If you refuse to give up your insanity, your little personality flittings, this will be your room."

I take a step back, doubling over. I can't help but feel his words like a punch to my stomach. He can't be serious! We can't stay in here. We'll die if we're left in this cell. "You wouldn't leave her here…" My words are breathy and no more than a plea. I'm gulping air, trying to still myself but failing miserably. Get ahold of yourself, dammit!

"I would, and I will." I see his shoes come into view as he grabs my chin and forces me to stand up straighter. "I won't tolerate your insanity any longer, Gillian. You will behave and conduct yourself properly."

Breathing shallow, hard breaths in through my nose, tears fall despite my will to stop them. "She can't..."

He shakes my head, digging his nails into my cheeks. "She can. She will. She has no choice." He lets go of my face but steps into my body. Forcing me into a tight embrace, he lowers his voice. "Okay, here's your choice, Gilli. Stay here and stay insane, or come back upstairs with me and be what you were always meant to be. Mine."

I want to push away. I want to claw and chew my way away from him, but I know that would be a mistake. I learned long ago that I'm no match for him. And inside a locked cell? We can't stay here!

I lower my forehead to his shirt. Hot tears fall, and I no longer try to stop them. Defeat should always be accompanied by mournful tears.

His lips press against my head, pushing me down into him more. "You will be my wife in four short months. Right after you graduate, my love, we will wed. I told you I would always take care of you." I feel his hot breath and try to match mine to his because I can feel my knees wanting to give from lack of oxygen. "I know you can do this. For me, you can stop your childish intemperance and give yourself over completely."

I stop a laugh, hiding it with the shaking of my body against his. It takes me a moment to be able to respond with a weak protest. "We didn't choose to be this way. We just are. You can't force us to be what we're not."

He pulls me gently off his chest, holding me at arm's length. The look on his face is so calm, so reassuring, that for a moment I'm soothed by it. But then insanity comes tumbling out of his mouth, in an equally calm and assured manner. "If I can't force you to be exactly what I want, then I will force you to spend the rest of your days in here, alone and locked up, because that's what happens to crazy people, Gillian. They. Get. Locked. Up." His gleaming smile is the picture of madness.

I shake my head but words freeze. He doesn't give me a chance to speak anyway; his fingers dig into my arms. "I want my answer from Gillian, or I walk out this door and give you a week to think about it."

Panic flutters my heart, but it's Grace that will have to speak for us. I back away onto the stage, staring in disbelief at the sweet and loving look on Miles' face.

I never believed he would be that cruel to Grace. To me and the rest of us? Sure, but not to her. It was a foolish mistake. But his words rang true then. We understood from Mother's threats how easily we would find ourselves locked up by the sane, unchanging world. She had made it clear that if we ever exposed her brutalities, she would make sure we never saw the outside world again.

Miles was just putting a new spin on her old threat. We knew he'd keep his promise the same as Mother would have.

He sneers at me, and I blink away tears of frustration at showing him any emotion now. "Enough games, *Gillian.* You've had your fun. Now it's time we have a serious talk."

I know what he's trying to do. It's what he's always done. He means to usurp me and bring Grace to the forefront. It's always her that he wants. I can feel the ping in my head, small and half-hearted. Grace doesn't want to face him. I can also feel the fear from her and the others. It's a loud drum, in time with my heart rate, that threatens to drown out everything else. My own fear at being this close to him again is nothing in comparison.

But we're not trapped in a locked room this time, and I've promised myself to never show him that fear again.

"You're stuck with *me*, Miles. *I'm* not going anywhere." I force my feet to move, to spread a little wider under my dress. I jut my hip out more and cup it with my hand. Tossing my hair back, I hope I look stronger than I feel. "And there's *nothing* you can do about it." I got through that without blinking. Ha!

A lot can happen in a heartbeat though, even a really fast one. Lives crumble. Promises are lost.

He chuckles and steps closer, putting his hand on my waist right above mine. I can feel the warmth of his touch and start to recoil, but his fingers tighten. "You'll either cooperate and leave with me now, or your *host* will be seeing the inside of a jail cell within the hour."

I don't want to understand what Miles is threatening, but I do and all too clearly in that one heartbeat. "You wouldn't." My voice burns out of my throat, the words acid I wish I could use to hurt him. His smile stretches even more as his fingers cinch painfully into my waist.

"Try me." He leans forward, and his familiar aftershave fills my mouth with the fear I gulp down. "Come out, come out, wherever you are." His singsong whisper brushes hot air against my cheek with each word.

And I give in; I go. Grace is what Miles wants. She's pretending to be brave enough to face him, but we all know the score now. There's no winning with him. Not tonight. Not here.

I can just see Miles leaning back; I can just feel his hand relaxing on my waist as I turn around in our mind and retreat into the darkest corner.

I'll live in the heartbeat before this one. I'll live in the moment that held all the hope and happiness I had with Simon. I'll live in the one where my promise was kept and I didn't show any fear.

I won't abandon Grace, but she'll have to find the courage on her own to face Miles now. Courage she barely had three years ago.

Anderson Valley: Grace/Gillian

It's always a little disorienting to be out at first, to take the stage from another. When we were younger, before we had even imagined the stage as a stage, it was worse. I would black out for seconds or minutes before becoming conscious of my physical surroundings again. This resulted in a lot more bumps and bruises as a child. Of course, those injuries paled in comparison to the ones we already had from Mother, and I never felt them anyway.

It was when I was five and Mother took me to see the Nutcracker that I first started to imagine a stage in my head.

I pictured myself in the center with a big spotlight on me. I didn't move like the dancers had on the stage that Christmas. I stayed still in the warm light, but I could safely watch all that happened in the outside world from that spot.

I pictured the others too. I couldn't really see them clearly as it seemed they stayed in the darker edges or behind curtains. We knew about each other before then, partly anyway, but on the stage, we started to see each other more distinctly over the years. And our number grew to five. I think there are others, but they choose to stay so far back from the light that we never see them. We don't know them. We only hear them sometimes.

Gigi, the one Simon likes to call Red, has seen every dark corner beyond the stage. She's fearless in her explorations, but she won't tell the rest of us what she finds, or who. It's probably for the best. I don't think we really want to know. The darkness we've each seen outside is bad enough for us.

Turning away from the stage and the heat from the light above, I can concentrate on the outside more. I can force myself to be a part of the physical world without blacking out or missing a beat between another's retreat. We've all perfected this, having learned through necessity not to leave our body unguided or unguarded for any length of time.

I become aware of our physical body as always. It's not like awakening from a dream, but more as emerging from a pool of water. Waves of sensation ripple across my skin. It's the tingle in my toes against a strap of leather, a coolness of fabric against my legs, an itch from a hair moved by the air against my cheek, and the heat from a body held too close against mine. I become aware of all of this in waves.

I look down first, too afraid to look up yet. I see Miles' strong and elegant hand on my waist. I see his fingers squeeze slightly before registering the increase in pressure on my body.

"There's my sweet Gilli." His deep and melodic voice is also a wave I can feel from head to toe.

I look up enough to see his lips. They're parted in a smile, his teeth just showing, and I watch as his tongue pushes out and wets the surface. I admire how the petal pinkness glistens in the romantic lighting. I lick my own lips in response, and Miles grins more. "I knew that would get your attention. You wouldn't want to make any trouble for your new *friend*, would you?" I shake my head, not taking my eyes off his lips now. I let a deep breath out as the sneer that accompanied his emphasis fades. "Good. Sex trafficking can be such a messy charge to get out of, especially when there's so much evidence to be found so easily."

It only took a moment for Miles' threat to register with each of us, only a second to come to a decision that we've run from for three years. *My* decision ultimately, but it's one we will all have to live with in the end.

His lips smile again. I've been able to read whole volumes of emotions from just watching his mouth. I know if he's happy, sad, angry or anxious from even the smallest movement of those two perfect petals. And it takes every bit of willpower to stay standing under the force of the dread they elicit now. There is no end to the rage his lips hold back with that deceptively charming smile.

The choice of my own freedom at the cost of Simon's is no choice at all, not for me anyway. It still takes every bit of strength I've managed to gain over our brief years of independence to stay on the stage, alone and pressed to Miles.

It's thoughts of strength that make me do something foolish. I look up into his eyes to say what we need to say. They are just as I remember them, glinty, fathomless pits that match his smile, all charm and beauty, all rage and fury. His anger is obvious at my lack of submission in looking directly into his eyes now, but I manage to hold on to the small amount of courage I have while I'm still able to. "If I go with you now, Miles, will you leave…him alone?" I'm not foolish enough to dare say Simon's name. I could see the narrowing of his eyes at just the thought of his name passing through my lips. I lower my own eyes quickly back to Miles' mouth, watching as it jerks up into a sneer.

"Of course, my love. You may consider it your *homecoming* present." My knees buckle at these words, but his hand helps to stop me from moving.

I retreat onto the stage a little to steady myself, to get out what I need to say next. I know I'll pay for this, but it has to be done. "I'll need to say goodbye to him…so he doesn't look for me."

The smile and hand tighten at the same time. "How thoughtful of you. I'm sure *he'll* appreciate not being left to wonder what happened to you." He doesn't need to say that it was his fate to wonder when Gigi ran three years ago, taking me away from him. His smile relaxes a little. "But don't think of trying to get away from me again. I have eyes everywhere, and you're leaving here with me tonight one way or another."

I can only nod my agreement, too afraid to trust my voice.

Glass shattering startles my attention away for a moment. The anger and betrayal so clear on Simon's face sends me racing further onto the stage, my false courage stripped away completely.

I barely feel Miles move his hand and turn around. I'm too busy falling face first onto the stage, weeping in fear, pain and relief at getting away. Gigi takes my place quickly, but I know it'll only be a brief respite this time.

Anderson Valley: Simon Lamb

I grab Red's wrist and pull her with me to a darker corner of the riddling room. Shielding her from view and trying to keep my voice lowered, it's through gritted teeth that I address her, "What the fuck do you think you're doing, Red?" My hands clutch her upper arms and shake her almost off the floor. I'm a man possessed, but I'm running on pure nerves right now.

She's impervious to the pain, as always, but there is something in her eyes I've never seen—almost pain, almost fear, almost sadness? "What were you doing talking to that man, letting him touch you like that after I *ordered* you to stay away from him?"

She doesn't move away or even wiggle in my tight grip, but her eyes burn with anger, smoldering out whatever other emotion she was hiding. "You're not the boss of me, Trust. I'll talk to anyone I want." My hand itches to slap her. She feels my fingers twitch and looks down and up quickly with her challenging smirk.

"Watch how you talk to me, Red. I haven't taken you to the cave where I've tortured many a girl before you, but I won't hesitate to take you there tonight if you keep this up." Her face flinches at this. I can't tell if it's the reminder of girls before her or the threat of torturing her, but it got her attention at least.

"So what? You'd treat *us* just like another one of your little sex slaves, Simon? You think *I'm* afraid of what *you* could do to me?" She thinks reminding me of her other selves—the ones that I could never harm—will break my anger, but I'm beyond thinking about anything right now except my blind obsession and crazed possessiveness.

"I'm not playing here. This is your last warning to start behaving, Red. No. Fuck that." I stand up, letting her arms go. "Get Grace." I regret saying it the moment I see the look in her eyes though. I know I just broke her unspoken cardinal rule—no demanding personality switches.

She flashes a second of pain and more of that something else I can't figure out, but it's gone in the next blink of her eyes. She laughs one sharp breath out and swallows hard. "Too bad. *She* doesn't want to see you either, Trust."

"Everything okay over here?" I turn a little at Cary's whispered voice behind us. I know how this must look—a crazy man making a scene. Grandfather would be so proud.

I let Red push me out of her way, and she storms off to the bathroom. Before turning around, I take a deep breath and brush both hands across my face. "Yeah, everything's just great, cuz. Let's get a drink."

Anderson Valley: Red/Gigi

Staring into a mirror is always a unique experience for me. I've aged with this body. Grace has as well, so it's not that. I know it's more difficult for Lilly, Baby and Jill. They've not grown up physically. They avoid mirrors altogether.

But viewing my reflection always takes a moment for my eyes to communicate to my brain that it's *me* I'm seeing. The doctors said it was unusual for me to have both such a strong sense of self and an awareness of the inconsistencies in our existences. I guess they expected that I would just override what I see in a mirror to match what I actually am. Grace does this; she only sees a reflection of herself the same as we all see her on the stage.

But I am fully aware that this is a body I share with others. I know the dark haired, dark eyed beauty in the reflection is me as everyone else sees us, but I also know that I'm taller and shapelier in reality. I know my features are more exotic, and my eyes are more interesting with flecks of caramel mingling with the chocolate. When I look in a mirror, I see two faces staring back at me, one more like a watermark than the other.

Looking at the bathroom's mirror now, I'm not seeing either version of myself though. My eyes are too blurred with angry tears.

Three years of freedom and it's all I'll probably ever have. I squandered it, and I shared it with the others. I made good on my promised plan. We each had our time on the stage. I even gave Grace and Lilly their own home and that crappy job in Castro to feel safer. They thought I was foolish for keeping such a nice place in Potrero and splashing my photos around the city.

I knew that I had covered my tracks though. I didn't tell them that I only planned on staying in San Francisco for a few more months. The name I'd chosen for us, Grace Martin, would have disappeared again, never to be reused. I made the name up to help ease Grace out from the corner of the stage and because Martin Vanderson was the only kind man I'd ever known.

That was before we met Simon. I was foolish to think that disappearing within the walls of his home would be good enough. I let myself fall into the trap of feeling safe with him.

Now it's all over. And it's *my* fault. *I* promised to protect us, and all my planning, running and hiding were for nothing. They came to nothing, except more fear, more pain.

I know all too well that Miles will be maniacal in his wrath and retribution, and I won't be able to protect poor Grace this time.

But I *can* protect Simon at least. He has his faults, but he shouldn't have to pay for my mistakes. He shouldn't have to suffer for my foolishness.

I wipe away the last of my tears, annoyed with myself for letting them fall at all. I can't afford to show any weakness right now.

I take out the folded card I grabbed off a table. One side has the night's events and highlighted wines; the other side is blank except for the winery's logo. There's not much space in which to break a man's heart.

Less *is* more, I guess.

Holding my breath, I start the short and not so sweet note.

Anderson Valley: Simon Lamb

"So what's going on with you tonight?" Cary led me to a quieter corner in the next room, away from the barrels and tables, while he went for more drinks. I've kept my back to the crowd of people, but I can feel eyes on me still. The coolness of the room only serves to accentuate the heat in the pit of my stomach.

I take the glass of offered wine from his hand. "Nothing." His frown deepens at the sharpness of my tone. "Sorry. It's not you."

"Scarlet?" He barely whispers her name, like he doesn't want to set me off again.

I barely nod in response, not wanting to say any more on the subject either. I take the opportunity to take a big drink instead.

"So..." Cary's embarrassment is almost as bad as mine. "Wanna tell me why you're so worked up about a girl I didn't even know existed until tonight?"

I square my shoulders and look down the two inches I have over him. "Nope."

"Have it your way, cuz." He takes a big drink too. "I'll let you get back to your fun then. Me? I plan on pissing away some of your not-so-hard-earned money on a couple of barrel options and impressing a few on-their-way-to-drunk girls I spotted earlier." With that, he downs his glass and turns away.

That was his non-subtle reminder of the orgy that ended last year's event. The entanglement of legs, arms, pussy and ass *was* a lot of fun, but that was before I met a woman who had my insides twisted and tangled around *her*.

How have I let myself get so fucked up over one girl in such a short amount of time? I laugh quietly; it's not really *one* girl. I can imagine the look on Cary's face if I tried to explain *that*.

I really need to take some time to think through all this. Since seeing Grace for the first time, then losing her all those months ago, then discovering her again—and her secrets—I haven't had any time to really think about what to do. I've only acted on instinct and desire.

It's crazy to think that anything can come of this, right? I mean, I can't *really* be thinking that I could make this work with her. With *them*.

But I know how useless it sounds even to me. Whatever time I had to make up my mind is long gone.

Grandfather had warned me that allowing my impulsiveness and obsessions to lead me could end in nothing but trouble. The old man is probably laughing his ass off at me right now. Fuck. But I think he would've liked her—*all* of her, or at least the part that doesn't put up with my bullshit.

Sighing heavily and finishing the wine, I feel a little clearer, almost calm enough to deal with Red again. Hopefully she's calmed down too.

I smile thinking about how angry she looked. I wonder how she'd look naked, stretched out with a bar between her legs, arms pulled tight over her head, and that fire of anger in her eyes. She's been defiant before, but angry could be a whole new side of fun for us.

Anderson Valley: Simon Lamb

"I think your girl wants to kiss and make up." I've been searching the crowd in the main room for Red, but only found Cary in the middle of a group of women, all swaying and pressing against him. Asses bouncy, lips glossy, and eyes glassy—they're just his type.

He pulls his arm from around one girl's shoulders and reaches for his jacket inside pocket. "Scarlet asked me to give you this. Made me promise not to look at it." He hands me one of tonight's printed itineraries, now tri-folded. "Is it directions to a secret rendezvous, cuz? Can I join for being the messenger boy?" He snorts back his laugh as I give him a black look before unfolding the thick cardstock.

One glance at the short note and my heart sinks. "When did she give this to you?" My words are wooden, and my tongue feels too big for the desert my mouth's become.

Cary sits up straighter, moving his arms off both girls at his sides. "Just a few minutes ago. Why? What's wrong?"

"Which direction did she head in?" I can't swallow; I can barely breathe.

"That way." Cary nods and twists towards the main doors. He's standing now despite the languid arms pulling at his chest and pants. "Is something wrong?"

I hardly hear him as I'm racing to the doors. I manage not to knock anyone out of my way but just barely. My shoes slide and squeak against the hard floor, coming to a stop just outside.

I register my heartbeat and the faster staccato of my breathing, but the headlights and flash of jewelry only dim against the certainty that Red's gone as my eyes rake through the small crowd outside.

I lost her. Again.

I *fucking* lost her.

I close my eyes, and all I can see is the look on her face when I demanded that she switch places with Grace.

Through a tunnel, I can hear Cary behind me. "Simon? Simon! You all right?"

I shrug off his hand on my shoulder, still clutching her note in my fist. I didn't think I'd find her out here, but I had to try. I know from experience that when Red wants to disappear, she's pretty good at it. Fuck.

Anderson Valley: Red/Gigi

Dead woman walking. That's the phrase that clicks along with my heels towards the waiting car.

I take in the smug smile on Miles' lips and how his hands are clasped in front of him. He looks like a child attempting to contain his glee at being handed his favorite toy. There's a man to his right. He's shorter, stockier and alert to every movement, but he's not making eye contact with me. A third man stands just as hulking and rigid on the other side of the car.

Before my steps can reach the gravel drive, I take one deep gulp of air and hold it, swallowing down the smell of jasmine on the night as it mingles with the wine and bile threatening to bubble up my throat. I indulge in one last peek at the sky, memorizing the twinkling stars and a breeze's soft touch.

This is the last effort of a condemned woman to bear witness to her own existence. I capture the feeling of being here, being free, because in a moment, I won't be. I may never be again.

All efforts lost and locked away, only a small scratched patch of stage awaits my future days. It will be that or a locked cell in a hidden tunnel that time will forget.

I push my shoulders back, toss my hair and release my breath. I'm not one to be maudlin for long. I'll leave that to Grace.

I've lived in lesser moments than this, memorized them to sustain me through bleaker times. I can do this.

I only hope Grace finds the same strength. Poor girl, she's going to need it if she feels the memory of her last night with Miles the same as I do. My knees almost give with the remembered sound of her shirt tearing.

"I don't want to be left in here, Miles." Grace's voice is small but seems to reverberate off all the hard surfaces in the room. It echoes onto the stage.

Miles tilts her head up. "I know that, my love, but that's not the same as giving me your decision. If, and I do mean if, you leave here, it will be as you are now, not as a different personality. You will not hide away from your punishments or anything else. You. Me. Us. Always." He kisses her nose like he used to do when he was first finding a way to be near us, before he discovered how easily he could have exactly what he wanted with little effort. And Mother's help.

Grace sobs in once, but we all encourage her to be strong. Lilly and Jill almost scream their words to help her say what she must. It works because she's finally able to stop crying long enough to look up at him, or at his lips anyway. "Yes."

"Yes? Yes what?"

She swallows and tries again, but her throat catches and she coughs through a few more sobs, spitting the words out hysterically. "Yes...I'll do what you want...I'll be what you...please...just let me out of here!"

Miles' arms circle hers, soothing her back with gentle strokes as he hums into her hair how happy he is with her decision. They stand like that for so long that all of Grace's tears are spent, and she only leans against him finally.

Baby crawls away, her own tears not stopped. Lilly, Jill and I are left staring at each other, unsure of what to do now. I don't think we truly believe in this silence that we'll be stuck here, or that Grace will be stuck there, but I saw the look in Miles' eyes. I know he's determined. And he's mad as well. My thoughts race in every direction to figure a way out of this.

I'm so distracted that his voice actually startles me. "I'm very happy that you've come to this decision, Gilli. I knew you could be my brave girl." He moves with her in a slow waltz deeper into the room until her back bumps against a wall. "But you'll understand, I'm sure, that I need to be certain you really can do this. For me. For us."

My sinking fear is nothing compared to what Grace feels as Miles turns her to face the wall and gently lifts her wrists to be trapped in two cuffs, unnoticed a moment before. Stretched up on her toes, her head thrashes from side to side to try and see him behind her. She's so close to the wall that her hips bump against it with each twist.

"You need to stay still, my love." Miles laughs softly, his voice somewhere near the bed now, I think. "I don't want you to hurt yourself before we even get started."

I can think of nothing to do that will help Grace but counting deep breaths in and out, telling her to only listen to my voice. Lilly joins me in encouraging her to even her breathing out to match the pace I'm setting for her. If Grace keeps hyperventilating and thrashing around, she'll pass out, and I'll be forced to take over. I have no idea what Miles would do to us then.

Being locked in this room is not an option though. I repeat this phrase a few times, in a steady, hypnotic tone. This seems to calm Grace a little. Lilly picks it up like a chant, and soon Grace is only shaking slightly.

This seems to please Miles. His hand on her neck causes her to jump, and her shoulder fires with pain at the jolt, but she hisses through it. Her scream follows the rip of her shirt as it's torn from her back though, and her breathing is lost in panic once more.

Miles waits for her to calm again. We can't see him, but we know the familiar sound of a whip sliding against a floor. He must have hidden it under the bed, or in the gloom, we just couldn't see what was in plain sight. Either way, there's no mistaking what he plans now.

"I know that I've never really had the pleasure of hurting you before, Gilli. I know that all those times with your mother or me, it wasn't you." The crack against the wall to the right of Grace has her screaming, even though her back is left untouched. "I know that you've never really felt before what I'm about to do to you." There's another crack to her left, and her voice is already wearing thin from straining. "And it does please me to know that only I will ever have you this way, my love. That after all those times I had to share you with Anya, this will be a fresh start for just you and me."

Jill jumps to take over, but Lilly and I hold her back. There's no point in showing anger against Miles' torture. Jill would be just as trapped in the cuffs and this room with the maniac as Grace is now. Our only hope is for Grace to have courage and for this to be over quickly.

But Miles is prolonging the inevitable, enjoying drawing this out. And we're all powerless to stop him, powerless to help. "Being locked in this room is not an option," I whisper, picking up the chant again.

"And you'll feel everything this time, my love, because if you don't, if you run from here back into that little messed up brain of yours, then I'll leave you here, and I won't come back until you're ready to face your punishment. You're not leaving this room until you've proven to me that, no matter what, you'll stay My. Sweet. Gillian."

When he does start, and the whip finally falls on her back, even I forget to breathe. I forget everything except the sound of the crack, the feel of the burn, and the shake of her cries. In this tight of a space, I wouldn't think that Miles could get as much force behind each blow, but he does. He's had a good deal of practice to make every inch of the whip count, and he doesn't stop with a few lashes. His grunts continue to follow the snap just before the leather bites into her back over and over.

And when it's done, when he's panting behind us, Grace no longer cries out. She stopped screaming some time ago. But screams would have been easier to take than the incoherent sobs that escape her shredded throat now. Or the animal grunting from him as he moves closer and pushes her pants off, pulling on her arms that barely bear her weight anymore.

Or the sound of his pants dropping with the whip to the hard floor right behind her.

Or the feel of his tongue lapping over the open gashes on her back.

Or the feel of his hands rubbing the warm stickiness of her blood into her back, stomach and finally down into the hair and space between her legs.

Or the feel of his hardness as he rubs himself against her back, just before entering her roughly where he's never taken her before, her blood only making it a slightly easier violation.

She has no more screams for this new pain, only more whimpers, more incoherent sobs.

And it's easier to take now that her mind has given up trying to hold on, now that she's numbed to the pain.

I continue my steady walk to the car, to Miles, reliving the memories of the rest of that last night with him. He'd carried Grace back through that lit tunnel to her bed. She'd passed out, but I stayed on the stage that time, not wanting to risk angering him, not wanting to waste Grace's sacrifice like that.

I was the only one around when he whispered a kiss on her tear-stained cheek and told her how much he loved her. I didn't even laugh, too numb from rage.

I waited up all night for the opportunity to get us away from Miles. And here we are, right back in his arms.

Anderson Valley: Miles Vanderson

The anticipation of this moment has been too difficult for it to be over too quickly, so the drawn out nature of Gillian's walk to me now is fitting. Her small steps crunching their way to me make the perfect soundtrack for this moment. I can hear her hesitation, her unwillingness, with each slow drop of her foot. Yet, still she comes to me. I've waited to have my life righted again, suffered too long with the upheaval her disappearance caused.

I devour everything about her unhurried approach, even if it isn't my Gillian. Yet.

The sway of her hips push the length of red silk back and forth; it's mesmerizing and suggestive. The dip in the front is a bit much for my taste, the expanse of creamy smooth skin and soft swelling breasts a little too exposed. But I know this isn't a dress Gillian chose, so I can excuse it.

I smile as she gets closer. I can be magnanimous in all that I can forgive, so long as she plays nice and follows *my* rules. I know my Gillian will. I know in my heart that it wasn't *she* who left me.

I close the small distance to meet her, pulling her into my arms and pressing her to my chest. The rapid flap of her heart is a hummingbird against my suit jacket. She keeps her arms to her sides but doesn't resist my embrace.

A car door opening behind us is the final click to the soundtrack. I feel her lungs expand with a deep breath in; I can hear the little hitch in her throat before she slowly releases it. I don't need to look down into her eyes to know that she's changed. Already, I can feel her body yielding to me more.

I press my lips against her hair. "We'll never be apart again, my love." My Gillian brings her arms up to my sides, not quite reciprocating, but it's an acknowledgement nonetheless.

In Flight: Miles Vanderson

Gillian pulls herself into the leather seat more, tucking her legs under the skirt of her dress and twisting her upper body towards the window. Her arm and hand covers the gash of exposed flesh at the front of the garish dress.

From the start of our drive in the car punctuated by sharp commands from Spencer to his men, to waiting for our take off now, she hasn't spoken a word. Her eyes have barely made contact with mine. But she's been responsive, obeying only the slightest instructions from my fingertips to get in the car, to walk up the steps to the plane, to take her seat. She's silent but obedient, just as I remember her.

I pull off my suit jacket and drape this across her front, pushing it behind her shoulders so it stays in place. Her lips curl into a small smile, but only her chin lifts up to me. Her eyes remain on the darkened night outside my plane.

"Look at me." Her eyes reluctantly follow her head back up. I cup her chin and fold my upper body over the space she's tried to create with her distant stares. "Have you forgotten your manners, Gilli?"

Her gulping swallow pushes my hand with her chin. "Thank you." She has such a sweet, soft voice, tiny against the whirring start of the plane.

I let her go and sit on the chair facing hers. She doesn't take her eyes off me now. I can't tell if she trembles under my coat or only feels the movement of the wheels against the runway. Either way, I'm turned on. Her beautiful, dark eyes never waver.

I see the flight attendant heading our direction and wave her away. "I don't want us to be disturbed, my love. But, please, let me know if you need anything."

"Thank you, Miles." Her lips barely move, but hearing my name from them again after all this time is enough to make my cock spring up. I can feel the painful pressure pulsing against the seam of my crotch, and I like it. I never get as hard as I am now except with her.

"I think we should clear up a few things before we're home. Don't you?" She only nods and blinks rapidly. Her blush and lipstick stand out a little more against the paling of her face.

I have had plenty of time to think about what I would say to her when I found her at last. I've revised it over the course of the years, as her disappearance changed from a possible kidnapping to an obvious slap in my face, but all those words come down to one. "Why?"

She stops all blinking. I can see her eyes take on the subtle emptiness that indicates her withdrawal into herself. It's quickly changed into a look of aggression and challenge. Her cheeks flame with a barely bottled rage. "*Why*? You ask *why*?" She laughs and leans forward, my jacket slipping from her shoulders. I can't stop my eyes from caressing her. "You know why, Miles. *I* had to get her away from *you*." She nearly yells this at me over the increased engine purr.

I smile and am pleased to see her sit back in her seat again, an unconscious submission on her part to the fear I know she's trying to hide.

I wait until we are in flight to continue our conversation. She's turned away from me again. Her eyes and jaw are set in angry profile, but her fingers tap nervously on her leg.

I know this version of her well. She feigns invulnerability, but she can't keep it up for long. Like an animal pinned in a trap, she'll try everything to get free. Eventually, though, she wears herself out and lies down for her inevitable end.

I have only to close my eyes, and I can see the first time I truly knew this side of her. It was the first time I became fully aware of her splintered identities. I'd noticed funny things about her from the start and saw her mother studying me whenever I was around her, but once I saw the truth, I was amazed that I hadn't seen it sooner.

I lean back more, stretching my legs wider with palms flat on my knees, and continue to smile at her. "Do you remember the first time I told you that I knew you were different?" I can see that my question surprises her. She's unable to keep her coy and calm look in place for a moment, turning to face me again.

"Yes. Of course I do." She removes my jacket, folding it over the arm of her chair, before moving to cross her legs. The slit on her dress falls open even more. I'm able to keep my eyes on her face this time, even when she runs her fingers along her thigh and up past her breasts to rest on her throat. I can see that she meant to hide her need to swallow her fear down so she can continue in a steadier voice. "The roses had just been trimmed, and there were petals still on the ground."

I smile at her depiction; this side of her was always poetic. "I still can't smell a rose without thinking of *you*."

She bends her head, looking up seductively through her lashes. "Then why did you try to get rid of *me*?"

I ignore her question. "I saw you heading out to the gardens from my window that day. I was curious about why you would choose to go there with a storm threatening and after all the flowers had just been cut down. You never told me why."

She sits up more, weighing an inner dialogue about sharing anything with me. The part of her most hidden wins out, and she can't help herself but give in. "I liked the idea of thorny things growing back stronger after they were cut down. I wanted to see for myself." Her wistful sadness drapes her words in even more poetry.

"That was also the day I promised to keep you safe from your mother, as long as you didn't keep any secrets from me again." The hint of reprimand is unnecessary; my voice is sufficiently chilled. She's been keeping lots of secrets from me, but that ends today.

I was hoping for a crack in her ice at my words, but she only calmly blinks. Her lips are gently pressed closed, her silence a rebellion against all that I know she wants to say to me. "I'd suspected something before that, you know? I noticed the changing between your identities before then. And when I would touch." I stop. This is always the trick in having a conversation with the many sides of Gillian: how to differentiate between her personalities. I refuse to play her games though. The doctors said it was better to treat each one separately, but they didn't really know Gillian. They had no real clue how to free her from her warped and trapped mind. "When I touched and I could see that it would hurt, even when I was gentle."

She interrupts, "That wasn't *me*. I think you know too well that *I* don't hurt so easily." Her lips bow up in a small smile. "I remember that just as you walked up behind me, I was startled and pricked my finger on the stem I was holding." I return her smile slowly. I won't let her see the rise in my anger at her challenges. "Your mouth was warm around my finger, sucking on the tiny drop of blood. *You* never told me if you liked it." I lean forward to better emphasize my words over the plane's vibration while keeping my voice low, but she tosses her hair to the side and looks away, continuing before I get a chance. "Of course, I now know all too well that you like the sight of blood, so I suppose it's a moot point."

With my anger barely held back by a thread of my will, I try again to crack through her false front. "I remember thinking that you acted particularly peculiar on that day. When the thunder and lightning started, you pretended to be afraid, pressing yourself against me. And after the rain poured so quickly over us, it was *you* that suggested we make a run for the pool house." Her brows arch, but she doesn't turn her head to me. "*You* wanted to be alone with me."

Her head whips back, but she only presses her lips a little more tightly, not responding. "*You* wanted me to follow you out there, and *you* wanted me to touch you. *You* wanted me to know about your mental state."

"What *I* wanted is another moot point." Her voice shook a little that time, a small crack. "It didn't matter then, and it certainly doesn't matter now, not to you anyway, Miles."

"What matters to me is *Gillian*. It's all that's ever mattered to me." My own voice shakes with the conviction of this.

She lowers her eyes, and her hands cross as a wrap over her shoulders. Her voice is small, almost as sweet as my Gillian's but still deeper, huskier. "*I* never mattered to you at all?"

I wait until her eyes raise to mine before answering in a quiet, steady voice. "No."

She scoffs as a means to hide her tears, but her hands relax into her lap, and she smiles serenely at me. "Then you are a fool, Miles." She laughs harshly. "You really think that the girl you call Gillian will ever be what you want on her own? You nearly killed her! You are a bigger fool than even your father thought."

My hands are on her throat before I feel myself lift off the chair. I see the bulging of her eyes and veins as I squeeze my fingers around her. Her hands claw at mine, but I am steel against flesh with no release.

Finally releasing the breath I held in disgust, I shove her against the leather backrest and shakily sit down.

I force my limbs and back to relax into the seat as I watch her hands go to her stomach and throat simultaneously, coughing for air and glaring at me.

Control of my own breathing returns to me quickly, and I slowly smile.

In Flight: Red/Gigi

"You'll do well to think twice about deliberately angering me again." Miles smugly grins while the pops of light recede from the fringe of my tunneled vision. My throat burns with each gasp, but with my eyes, I try to convey the hatred I'm now too choked to speak. For the moment anyway.

The hand clutching my stomach, helping me to hold down the liquor I drank earlier with Simon, is also reminding me to swallow my anger, to hide it, hold it, bury it. I'll find a way to regurgitate this fury in my heart someday. It's a vow I make to myself.

I double over in my seat, a cramp clutching my stomach and tears threatening my eyes. I refuse to cry for him. That was a vow I made four years ago when he made it clear he didn't love *me*. I won't show him that he can hurt me, not ever again.

But the memory comes flooding back to me with a will of its own. It's a punishment for having trapped memories. I can't *not* remember something that happened to me in full sensory detail. The sights, sounds, smells, tastes, and most of all, the touches of every moment are always with me. Even the memories of the others that I've shared won't go away. I remember everything as if it happened only minutes before.

I can't lie to myself. The memory of Miles four years ago is one of *my* hardest to shrug off. It's as hard as the memory of that locked cell, as hard as the memory of Miles hurting Grace. It's a different kind of pain that I'm not immune to. Not a cut to my flesh but a slash into my heart.

Everything changed so quickly after Mother died, after Martin was no longer with us too. Miles didn't waste any time taking complete control immediately following their deaths.

In truth, he'd already taken control the year before when he joined Mother in her sadistic pleasures. That had just been a warm-up for what was to come though. Grace and I would both be devastated by him that last year living under his rule, her for his cruel treatment of her body and me for his cruel treatment of my heart.

"Gillian?" I smile up at Miles' stern face and take the hand he has held out for me. Uncrossing my legs, I rise from the library rug and follow his lead in silence to my bedroom. In the long walk, I rack my brain for what I might have done to anger him today, but I can't think of anything. Maybe he's had a hard day at the office and wishes to unwind with his whip.

He silently closes the door behind us, and I walk to my usual spot to await his mood, halfway between the door and my bed. Since he became my guardian last week, he hasn't punished me once. He's hardly touched me. Even Grace has not received much of his affection or wrath.

He turns around slowly, and an unfamiliar cold wash of fear splashes over me. His look is intense, as I've seen before, but his features are still refined. The slopes and angles of his strong bone structure aren't marred by any scrunching or frowning. He doesn't appear angry or ready to unleash his suppressed desires, but he's not smiling either, just staring at me.

Uncertain, I reach to pull my shorts down, and he finally breaks the silence. "No. That's not why I brought you in here." He comes to stand in front of me, taking my hands into his. "I brought you here to inform you of certain changes." The same cold wash, but this time it settles as a weight in my chest.

I risk speaking out of turn, "So much has already changed." I add a smile to show him my gratitude.

His lips only return my smile slightly. "Perhaps this would be a better conversation to have with, hmm, with a different you."

I'm hurt that he would ask me to leave, that he'd ask for Grace, but I smile more, wanting to please him. "All right, if that's what you want, Miles." I retreat onto the stage but stay close.

His smile brightens for Grace. So annoying! Why doesn't he see that she's just so boring?!

"There will be doctors coming to the house today." I push for Grace to ask him why, but as usual, she just waits for him to continue. She's so damnably docile! What does he see in her?!

His beautiful lips smile again, always so easily pleased by her submissive nature. "They're going to help you." He brings his hand up to brush the side of Grace's head and good pet that she is, she leans into it. She's practically purring when she should be asking him what the hell he's talking about. We're not sick.

Lilly and Jill come closer to me, feeling the tension filling the stage.

"They're going to help you to stay just as you are now." I shrug in reply when Lilly asks me what that means.

Grace finally succumbs to our united clamoring for an answer. "As I am now?" Her voice bounces off the stage, the fear a palpable thrum echoing louder.

"They're going to help you to be rid of your, er, personality issues." He lets go of Grace's hands and pulls her into a hug. The scent of cologne on his neck envelopes us. "You're going to listen and do everything the doctors tell you to. Then you'll be healed, my love. You'll be able to stay my sweet Gillian."

I can see the look of shock from both Lilly and Jill and know they can see the same on me. Grace only buries her face into Miles more, her response meek and whispered. "What if I can't do that?"

He pulls her back to look into her eyes, not seeing that she's already retreated back towards us. "Of course you can. And you will. You'll do this to please me."

I take advantage of her weak hold on the stage and push my way out. "What if we don't want to be 'healed' as you put it?"

His lips twist into his cruelest smile as his hands grip my arms. "You don't have a choice. You will be whole and healed and stay my sweet Gillian from now on. The doctors have assured me that it can be done."

I block the view of the stage without thinking. The noise from within is too much over the hammer of my heart. I lean into his chest, lifting my face just inches from his. I breathe in his warm fragrance and lower my voice as I know he likes. "Miles, we don't need a doctor." His fingers pinch into the soft flesh of my arms harder.

"This is for your own good, Gillian. For us."

I know I'm a fool for arguing when he's clearly holding back his anger, but I can't help myself. "Us? You mean you and her?"

"Yes."

My hands are on his chest, shoving him away so quickly that he's caught off guard and actually lets go of my arms with a step back. "And what about me, Miles? What about my love? You just want that to go away? You just want me to go away?" My voice rises with each question until I'm yelling at him in the end.

"Love? What love?" A slap would've hurt less. His words lash out, though, instead of his hands. I understand now why he hasn't touched us for the last week. Doctors will be examining us soon. "You debase yourself with a sick love of pain, and you think that will make me love you?" He laughs, and it's a kick I feel to my stomach. Though unlike the real kicks I've received before from him, this one hurts. "I love to punish you. Keeping you in line is what you need, Gillian. But watching you writhe around in ecstasy while I do it is not my idea of love. You're sick, and the doctors will make you well again."

Tears spring to my eyes, but I cover my face with my hands to hide them from him. He grabs my wrists and forces my arms down, bringing his face close to mine. "I won't accept anything less than 100 percent of you, Gillian. You will be exactly what I demand, and that means you will behave and follow the doctors' orders. You will be whole again."

I remember the feel of my wrists tingling from his touch; I remember the sound of the key turning in the doorknob as he locked me in; I remember the taste of salt as my tears rolled down into my mouth. And I remember the vow I made to myself to never let him see the rip in my heart.

When the doctors came, Miles informed them that I wasn't the "real" Gillian. I kept my tears to myself at that, but I stubbornly refused to leave. Three men and one woman were my judges, jurors and executioners. Maggots serve more purpose and were more pleasant than those four doctors. I was poked and prodded, mentally and physically, for hours. I don't think Grace could've handled any of it. I know the others couldn't have. Miles stayed for the whole thing, a cold, impartial mask on his face the whole time. I at least was able to contain myself and resist the urge to beg for a reprieve.

My hatred for him grew with each and every poke and prod though. Still, I was never able to completely rid myself of the love I had for him. Maybe my memory is to blame for that as well. The doctors said that having such a strong recollection of all my senses from every experience was part of the reason for my condition. It was a contributing factor in the splintering of my mind. I didn't stop laughing when they said that. My mind may not be like everyone else's, but who the fuck would want that anyway?

My resolve to stand against their interrogations didn't last long. Miles locked me in the bedroom and cut off all power and water for almost three days. I had no choice but to give in and pretend to cooperate.

I learned my lesson too though. Just as soon as I could, I made a copy of the key to the door off one I took from an unsuspecting maid. It was what made my escape possible a year later.

I was only happy he had locked us in our bedroom, not the cell that day. His overconfidence was our salvation, but it doesn't matter now. He won't make the same mistake twice, I'm sure.

I sit up more in the plane's cool leather seat, finally able to breathe without coughing. I may not have ever been able to divorce myself from my feelings for him, or rather the memory of those feelings, but I won't let Miles see that. I won't ever show weakness to him again.

The smile hasn't left his lips, and I allow my own to rise up the same way. My voice is more a hoarse whisper, but it's strong and that keeps me smiling. "You know *she* doesn't like to play rough like that." A tilted brow is his sole reply. "And yet you ask me why we left?"

"*She* didn't leave me. You did." I give him the same cryptic brow lift. His left cheek tics upward, a betrayal against the temper he holds in check with a tight grip. I'm barely able to stop a shudder that wants to bend my back with reminders of times when his anger wasn't kept bound. Hopefully, the plane hides my discomfort now.

My rebuttal catches in my throat though. It would only serve to put Grace at more risk. We're better off if he thinks I'm the only reason we stayed away. "Do you blame me? You threw me away, Miles."

"I only did what was necessary, what your mother and those specialists I hired were all unable to do. I helped you, *Gillian*." And I can see that he still believes this. The three years apart have done nothing to change his mind. If anything, he looks more convinced than ever by his own arrogance.

I counter my argumentative words with a softer voice, "You tried to force her to be what she never could, not even for you, and you forced me out the door to protect her." His sneer strikes a nerve of fear in my stomach but does nothing to detract from his handsome face. How am I still thinking he's handsome?

"She doesn't need to be protected from anyone except herself, and I'm going to do just that." He leans forward, and I follow the lines of his elegant fingers to my knee. The movement puts traces of his cologne on the bottled air, and I find myself leaning in too. I can't help but remember the first time I was wrapped in his scent and felt his warmth against me. I was so young and naïve then to think that he could be my hero, our savior.

His fingers remain still and gentle, but his voice takes on the harsher tone I know well. "I won't be making this *request* again. You, this side of her, all of her other sides will go away, starting now." I lift my chin but feel it starting to shake. Whether it's in anger or fear or some combination, I can't decide. "Or I will be forced to make good on my promise." He tilts his head, obviously enjoying my struggle to maintain control. "You do remember my promise, don't you?"

I take a deep, steadying breath. This *is* what I expected, but the finality of everything is still a hard blow to take. "Of course I do. We do." It was the promise of the locked cell that kept Grace in place through his brutal beating three years ago. It was being in the actual room that would serve as our prison if she didn't stay that gave her the strength to obey him that night. It was the threat of never seeing the light of day again, locked in that tiny closet of a space with no window, no escape, only the promise of a bowl of water and piece of bread each day that made her bear his abuse.

We never doubted Miles' willingness to see his threats through. It was Grace's bravery, in the face of our choiceless option, that made me follow through on my plans for escape the next day. She protected us that night by giving him what he wanted, and I protected us by running away as soon as I could. But we both failed, and we're right back where we started. Only now it's worse. Three years is a long time for a man to contemplate his obsession.

"Good, because I still have that room ready for you. I've added a few security measures as well. There will be no escaping this time." His lips part for a glowing smile, monstrous in its unbridled delight with himself. "Now, off you go." His head dismisses me with a nod into the air, like I'm a figment that can be displaced so easily with a wisp of wind. How did I ever fool myself into thinking that he loved me? That he loved Grace even?

I may very well have been a fool, but I was also an angry and hurt sixteen year old girl when I first made my plans for escape four years ago. He had broken my heart when he made it obvious that he only wanted Grace. I had no idea then the lengths he was willing to go to get what he wanted, but I waited one whole year before making good on my plan to get away from him. I waited until Grace finally understood that we had no choice but to run. I waited until Miles made his threat. I waited until he hurt her. I waited until she was as broken of her love for him as I was.

And I can wait again, in silent exile this time if I have to.

Because I'm not a fool anymore. I'm not a little naïve girl, looking to be loved at any cost. There really isn't any choice either. Miles isn't bluffing; his threats are all too real, both to lock us away and to hurt Simon.

At least this way, I can watch and hope for a second chance, keeping Simon safe in the meantime.

I won't give up though, and I won't let Grace either. I'll find a way; she just has to be strong enough to take whatever happens in the meantime, poor girl.

I turn inward, but instead of heading into the light of the stage to comfort the others, I move into the shadows. I seek out the hidden ones, knowing I'll gain strength through what they hide.

But when I hear Miles' voice as if from a distance, I have a thought that stops me in my tracks.

I don't actually know that Grace doesn't still love him. She answered "yes and no" when Simon asked her if she loved another. I know she meant Miles.

I turn back toward the stage but realize that it's too late, and it doesn't matter anyway. If she loves him or not, she'll still need to find the strength to be what he wants, and I must find a way to escape him again.

In Flight: Grace/Gillian

I feel Gigi brush by me. Her withdrawal is swift, and I know she's trying to stay strong even as she runs from Miles now.

I also know how insane that sounds.

I've always been aware of how crazy I seem. Hidden and sheltered on the stage, I watched the interaction between Gigi and Miles. I know what he expects. He thinks of "me" as crazy. His doctors all signed off on how certifiable I am.

Mother always used our insanity to threaten us into keeping her secrets.

Miles thinks the year with those doctors was enough to convince me that he's right though. He believes I'm the "real" Gillian and that I should be able to stay present at all times.

I'd laugh if I wasn't torn between wanting to scream and wanting to cry at the moment. It's ludicrous to think that I'd be strong enough to overcome the others and stay for longer periods of time. No matter how much Miles wants that, I've never lasted for longer than a few weeks outside. Lilly's actually been able to stay longer than I have.

This, more than anything, is what convinced me to follow Gigi's plan three years ago. I knew I wasn't resilient enough to live up to what Miles wanted…no, what he demanded. As much as I loved him, I knew I would never be enough for him, and I would never be strong enough to take the pain he needed to inflict.

I feared that we'd end up in that cramped room. No doubt, we really would go crazy if that happened. Not even Gigi had the strength to stay in that tiny cell.

I owed it to her and Jill and Baby and Lilly to keep us safe. I owed it to them to support her plan for escape, but in the end, it didn't matter. I can feel her hopelessness now like a cloud that shadows only part of the landscape. Or perhaps it's my own hopelessness I feel as I pull Miles' jacket back over me as a protective layer against his watchful eyes.

His voice is so low, so masculine, it's a gentle rocking to my body. "You rest for now, my love." I close my eyes and feel the tears slipping down my cheeks. They're hidden by my hair, and I'm grateful that the shame from the wetness between my legs is hidden too. I hate how I physically respond to him, even now.

A cold, detached thought springs into my head. Maybe it's better this way. At least I know that my body will give him what he wants, even as my mind thinks to refuse. I told Simon that I still belong to Miles, but he made me doubt that truth when I was in his arms. Now I see how foolish I was to think that I could ever *not* belong to Miles.

…But what about my heart?

I fly away from this thought, not onto the stage as I want but into the arms of a deep exhausted slumber, a blanket of darkness that will briefly protect me.

Anderson Valley: Simon Lamb

"I'm going to take off." Cary's voice is subdued and annoying as it echoes off the glass enclosure. It's been four days since Red ran from the party, and he's been hanging around here trying to be something he's not—my babysitter. I only nod in response, not moving my eyes from the reflection of shadows and light on the calm surface of the pool. "You need anything before I go?"

I don't turn my head. If I did, I'd tell him to fuck off or worse. "Nah. I'm good, man. I'll call you in a few days."

And because I can still feel his worry, heavy on me like the wet towel over my shoulders, I add, "We'll plan a night next week."

His feet shuffle with his weight bouncing back and forth. "'Kay. Anything you want, cuz. Take care, man."

He finally leaves, but I wait a few minutes before tossing the towel onto the table next to me and sitting forward with my head in my hands. Fuck.

It's all I can think. It's all I've been thinking for hours. Fuck. If I let my mind veer to anything else, I go into a blind rage. I take in a few deep breaths, letting nothing fill my head more than the intensified chlorine smell filtered between my fingers.

I finally get up, but my limbs feel heavy, soggy like my shorts. I hate sitting around in a wet suit; it makes me itch. Without thinking, I strip the shorts off, leaving them in a puddle on the tile.

I've always loved this pool. The calmness of the water is usually the perfect antidote to whatever bullshit obsession is battering my head. It didn't work today, but I still step into the water again. Marveling at the steady ripples, I do my usual count to see how long it takes for the waves off me to start pushing back against the far side.

I need this emptiness. After the darkness of the last few days, it feels good to be drained of any thoughts or feelings. I reach the bottom step and slowly lower myself into the pool, taking a lung full of air before letting the water lap calmly over my head. This is my favorite part—sitting on this step, submerged and holding my breath.

It reminds me of my grandfather and is a christening of sorts for me. When I came to live here, he brought me to this room first, telling me that I would learn to swim in this pool. He said there's no greater feeling for a man than using weightless resistance to overcome something that could destroy you. Swimming and flying are two things we're not meant to do, but man can transcend his limits and make anything possible—Grandfather's words, not mine, but they've stuck with me.

My first night here, I came down to this pool by myself, after all the lights went out in the house. I got lost on the way a few times, but that only made it more of an adventure and me more determined.

The first time I stepped foot in this pool, I was nude and shivering despite the heat from the water. It wasn't cold or fear that shook me though; it was excitement. I wanted to face the challenge my grandfather had presented. I wanted to be the man he talked about—the one he described in that strong voice graveled from decades of smoke.

And that first night, I went down the steps and stopped at the third one. The water was already up to my chest, as comfortable as a bath. I started my ritual of counting the seconds for the waves to start returning to me that night. When I was satisfied I'd conquered the tranquil surface, I slowly sat down, grabbing the railing to keep myself from floating up. I gulped my air down and squeezed my eyes shut, enjoying the feeling of being submersed in warm liquid.

I didn't count the seconds that I stayed under; I was too distracted to start another obsession. The bubbles that tickled across my skin demanded too much attention, as did the burning in my lungs so quickly after the hair on the top of my head started floating away from me. When I came up for air, I whooped a cry of victory with a jump and slipped on the step. I flailed with my little boy arms and legs pumping, swallowing mouthfuls of chemical water until finally my fingers brushed against metal and I was able to blindly latch on to the railing again, pulling myself to safety.

I hacked and sneezed water, fighting the need to throw up, but when I was finally able to breathe again, I was smiling. The water around me was still churning, and I could feel it waking against the step behind me, splashing water onto my back. It felt like a pat for a job well done. I waited until I could hold my breath again, and I sat in the water another five times, each time staying down a little longer.

I felt like a conquering hero that night, but I also gained a respect for what my grandfather had said. The water could have destroyed me, pulled me under and never let go. It felt good to resist that. I had some control over something for the first time in my very young life—a control that I was desperately in need of, then and now.

I saw that same need in Grace, in all her personalities. She became *more* to overcome what could have destroyed her, to take back some of the control she never had. I suppose a lot of people would think she is destroyed, split into five parts. I think it shows her strength—her determination to weightlessly resist what tried to pull her down.

Slowly standing, I enjoy the momentary lightheadedness and wait to open my eyes again. The simple blackness is broken only by the feeling and sound of water running rivers down my body. At least in this room, I can't imagine Grace or Red. I didn't get a chance to bring her here before she fucking left.

Getting out of the pool, I debate again my decision to give her some space, some time.

I wanted to run down the drive and search for her on the country road that night, but seeing the concern on Cary's face at the crazed one on mine was enough to knock some sense into me. The valets were useless, but I assumed that Red found a willing helper to give her a ride. I knew I wouldn't find her walking, that's for certain.

I snort. I'm sure Red found herself a nice ride, but I try not to think too long on that. I can distract myself with all the other ways she pissed me off instead.

I don't know if it's the fact that she left or left with only a short note that has me more enraged. I kept expecting her to show up. Not that I thought she'd come crawling back to me exactly; that's not her style. It's not Grace's either. I did think by now Red would come walking through my door with some smartass response ready though. Or maybe Grace would come back and ask for an apology in her quiet, sweet way.

But neither did, and I'm losing hope that either will.

So I have two choices, or three I guess. I can forget her—not really an option since I've tried it before and failed. Plus, I just don't want to. She's my obsession, and I'm too far gone now to give her up.

So that leaves me with finding her and forcing her back here. It's a thought that makes me feel oddly sickened, probably because it's just what Red accused me of before she left—treating her like one of my products.

I thought she knew that she was more than that to me. I thought she understood so much more than she did apparently. Or maybe it's her batshit nuttiness getting in the way. Or maybe it's that I crossed the line with demanding an identity switch. Whatever it is, I'll have to make her see what she means to me. If I can just get past the anger over her leaving.

I can imagine taking my rage out on her. I smile with the thought of Red in an elaborate twist of chains and ropes and leathers. I'd whip her once for every letter in her fucking short note, then start all over again.

But the reality of knowing that I'll have to deal with not only Red but Grace and the others? Fuck. I've never felt remorse before. It's disgusting.

Grace had said that I could love her or hurt her, but I couldn't break her; she was already too broken. She said I was broken too. Maybe I am because I promised not to hurt her but then treated her like she was just a product—threatened to toss her in my cave and torture her. Fuck, I even reminded her of all the women I've done just that to.

I can't blame her for wanting to leave, but I can't forgive her either. I sure as shit can't forget her. I'll give her a little more time, but eventually she'll need to come to terms with a simple fact. She's mine. Broken or not, mad or not, she belongs with me.

Which is why I've chosen option three—wait until she's cooled off before finding her. I don't like it, but this option at least gives me some hope that she'll return to me on her own. It's a hope that whatever fucked up relationship we were starting could work out between Grace, Red, the others and me. I just have no clue how to make that happen quite yet.

So I'm giving her space, giving her time and waiting. Fuck. I'm giving myself this space and time too. My anger hasn't subsided, and I hope she's having better luck because when I do find her—I let my threat stay unspoken, even in my own head. I have no idea what I'll do when I see her again.

I thought I needed time to figure this out, but now that I've had some, I know it's no use. There is no figuring out us. It is what it is. Red fuels my depravity, leaving me exposed and raw with the emotions she so eagerly reveals and desires; in the next second, Grace soothes my cravings, leaving me ripped open and vulnerable to the softness she so readily shares. It's everything I ever wanted and never knew I needed. I'm so fucking pissed off at her for throwing it all away with one fucking short ass note that I want to explode with the desire to find her and fuck the shit out of her.

My laugh bounces off the glass walls and ceiling. Yep, the image of fucking her has definitely taken over the thought of punishing her again.

Cary had suggested that we head back to the city. He thought a few sluts would be more than enough to take my mind off her. He didn't understand why I would want to wait around here. He was slick about it, but he kept prying for more information about her. I could see that he wasn't going to let it go. I finally gave up today and told him most everything. He at least didn't act pissed that I'd lied to him about her. He didn't act overly sympathetic either, which was good. That would've just sent me into another rage.

I didn't tell him about her personalities or that I was watching her over a year ago, and he didn't ask too many questions. It felt good to finally stop calling her Scarlet, though, and to have someone to talk to about her, even if I didn't say much.

He still doesn't understand why I'm staying and waiting. He knows I've never waited for anything, and I'm regretting my decision more each day.

A part of me is still hoping she'll come back on her own, like the waves that return to me on the water's surface. I just have to stay steady and count out the wait.

Seattle: Miles Vanderson

My fingertips find her first. I brush against Gillian's softness slowly, keeping my eyes closed and relishing the delight of trying to figure out what part of her I'm touching without peeking. She's still asleep, so I keep my fingers light.

Her flesh bumps as I slide the blanket down further. It's definitely her hip and thigh; I feel her bone and contours, the hard curve of muscle and smooth hairless skin. She quietly whimpers and twists as I open my eyes.

In the pale rising rays filtering in, I can see my hand over a large bruise on her outer thigh. It hasn't yellowed yet, a remnant from our first night reunited.

She lies on her side. The sheets snake around and under her arms and legs but do nothing to cover her. I watch her stomach rise and fall with her steady breaths. The hair between her legs is coming back nicely. She's still, so like the first time I saw her nude in her bedroom all those years ago.

She twists again in her fitful sleep, moaning as her back arcs away from me. Even with her hair covering most of it, I can still see the marks left by Lamb. The sight of those pale pink lines ignites the same furious response in me as it did only a few nights ago.

"Take off that whore's dress, Gillian. I've bought you something more appropriate for a bride to wear." The lights from the Vegas Strip stretch as vibrant threads in a dark carpet outside the large windows of our hotel suite. Not my ideal choice for our wedding, but I've had to wait long enough to have my bride. This brief layover will be a distant memory tomorrow when we start our lives as man and wife.

Picking up the simple white dress draped over the edge of the bed, Gillian turns to the door of the bathroom. "No. Undress here. I want to see you." There's a fevered lust coloring my words, but I see no reason to hide it now that we're alone.

She puts the dress back down gently, smoothing out the wrinkles in the fabric under the plastic covering. Turning to face me, she keeps her eyes demurely lowered. She knows how I like her sweet innocence.

In one slow movement, both her arms extend up and back: one to hold the dress, one to lower the zipper. My pulse races with the slow sound of the fabric letting go.

Three years I've waited for this moment, and I drink in every detail of her; but watching her pull herself out of the overly bright dress, I'm reminded of a butterfly shedding its cocoon. She's more beautiful than even my memories could ever hope to capture, and I won't have to live with only memories ever again. My butterfly is in my net, and she'll stay in it this time.

"Stop." She halts all movement: frozen on half-bent legs, fingers outstretched from releasing her dress to the floor, hair falling over her shoulders as a dark curtain. "Come to me, my love."

With her head still down, she obeys. My own breath can't match her steadiness, catching in my chest with the thick drumbeat of my heart. My hands actually shake reaching to pull her against me. I hope she understands how filled my heart is with her here now.

But reality has a cruel way of marring even the most perfect of moments. My fingers on her back find familiar ridges, reminders of her long absence and her time spent with another man. Her only reaction to my firming grip on her shoulders is a stiffening to her back. "You've been gone for too long, Gilli. I worry that you've forgotten how much I love you." My words are whispers against her head.

Her response is a soft murmur spoken into my chest, *"I haven't forgotten, Miles, and you show me now by finally making me your wife."*

My jaw works, clenching and unclenching, trying to keep control of the anger blazing through me. I keep my eyes closed tight, not wanting to see the evidence of her betrayal on her back. I don't respond until I'm finally in control more. *"You know how much I love you, yet you've let another man touch you."* It's not a question, not even an accusation. There's no point to a denial. I run my hand up and down her back to underscore my words.

"I...it wasn't me..." We both know she's lying though. I can hear it in how flat her voice is. She's withdrawing a little to keep herself from reacting, but it's obvious that she allowed Lamb to have his way with her. It's her nature to submit. The thought of her acting that way with another man frays the strained control I maintain on my temper.

"Turn around, Gillian." I let her go, but she stays close, pivoting so her back is to me with her head lowered. I push her hair away, and she remains still and quiet.

Her back is a beautiful canvas of pink and cream. Lamb knew what he was doing at least. There are no cuts, no lasting damage, just exquisite welts in a perfect pattern, none overlapping each other even. My blood boils in my temples, and a hiss of hot air escapes my lips as I run just one finger up the longest mark and she doesn't respond. That should've hurt her.

"You know my rule, Gillian." This produces a nice full-body response: a shudder to her shoulders, a weakening to her knees.

"Please, Miles?" There's no whine, no cry, just her same flat voice. She knows it's no use to argue with me. We went over this three years ago, the night before she ran away. Still, she turns quickly to face me, pleading with her large chocolate eyes, so soft and sweet. "Just for tonight. Please."

This being our honeymoon night, I might be moved by sentiment and allow her this concession just this once if she wasn't already marked by another. Now my anger, the rage I've held in check for three years, demands full payment though. I won't allow her to hide within herself and withdraw from the pain she knows she deserves, not tonight, any other night, or ever again. I explained this rule three years ago. I shake my head. "Now. Turn. Around." Her lower lip quivers, but she turns back.

Her mother didn't understand this. She didn't understand Gillian really. Anya knew about the personalities of course, but she chose to either ignore them or, sometimes, delight in them. She never tried to heal her daughter, not that I expect it even crossed her mind to try. Anya was the cause of Gillian's fractured state, and I think she reveled in knowing that most of all.

What Anya didn't understand was that without pain, discipline is a useless tool. Anya was crazy though. Very little about her daughter escaped her attention, but she didn't really care if Gillian learned a lesson from any of her punishments. She hurt Gillian because she enjoyed doing so; it amused her is all.

I want so much more for my Gillian. I won't allow her to hide in herself ever again. Her mother may have tolerated that behavior from her, but I've made it clear that I won't.

I pull her arms to bring her back against my chest, breathing in her hair. "I love you, Gilli."

"I love you, Miles."

Her voice is the same as that first time four years ago in the library when we declared our love for each other, soft and sweet. It's also edged now with pain from my jacket pressing against her raw back.

She stirs more and rolls over to face me, her eyes slowly opening. I smile watching her expression change from confusion, to blankness, to finally awakening in full awareness and presence again. Her brows knit together to form a small frown.

"Good morning, Mrs. Vanderson." I kiss her nose gently. It's still a little swollen, but the small bruise across the bridge is lighter. Her lips poke up into a smile, despite her brows lowering even more. "I have a long day scheduled in the city, so you need to get dressed and in your room quickly, my love. You'll have breakfast there again."

She pouts, which is pretty, but as a display of willfulness, it's not to be tolerated. She quickly changes into a more appropriate look, but her words reach for me as her hands do when I move to get up. "Please. I've been good. I've done everything you've wanted, Miles. Haven't I?"

I sit back against the headboard and slide her to me so her upper body rests on mine. It's true that she's been perfectly obedient, without a trace of her other selves or any attempts to hide within herself, since we left California four days ago. "And do you think it's good for you to question my orders now?" I run my fingers through curls made wilder by her restless sleep, my hands continuing down her back and sides with each stroke. I haven't made any marks to her back. I refuse to overlay what was left by Lamb. I can wait until her back is completely clear again to make my point of ownership on that part of her.

"No. I want only to know that I please you, Miles." I chuckle with this response. She thinks to twist me around her little finger. That may have worked before she ran, but I know I have a responsibility to keep her on a tighter leash now. It's for her own good.

"I'm very pleased now that you're back where you belong." I smile into her hair. I know it's unnecessary to remind her of why she's being punished, but I'm feeling self-indulgent this morning. "And I told you on our wedding night that you would be spending three weeks in your room as atonement. That's only one week for each year you kept me waiting. I don't think that's unfair. Do you?"

She responds quickly, "No. I want only to be with you. I'm lonely in that room without you." She keeps her voice small and sweet in an attempt to not anger me with arguing more. It's futile, and she should know that.

"I won't be here anyway, so you'd be lonely no matter what." I feel her move to speak again but cut her off angrily, "Think very carefully, Gilli, about what comes out of your mouth next. You haven't earned the right to be free. If you keep up with this line of questioning, you will spend the *night* in your room too." I don't like this, but I know that I will have to follow through on this promise if necessary. I would hate to have to spend the night without her, but she has to learn somehow.

"Of course. I'm sorry, Miles. I'll look forward to seeing you when you're home then." She moves to get off my chest, but I keep her pressed to me.

"And will you look forward to submitting to your punishment tonight as well, my love?" I've beat her every night, not as harshly as the first one but enough to break her to tears each time. It's just enough to sate my temper a little, and I told her that this will continue for three weeks. She'll spend her days in solitary contemplation of how she betrayed me and her nights in tearful retribution for it.

"I'll look forward to deserving your love again." Not quite the answer I wanted, but I can feel her body melting against me too. She knows how much I like when she gives herself to me completely.

Rolling us over, I hold her under me. I fight the urge to punish her more. I've made a promise to myself to not start a session unless I can devote a proper amount of time to it though, and my schedule this morning is not going to cooperate with my desires.

I pull back, and her face is red from being smashed against my shoulder. Her eyes try to hold back the pain I can so clearly see. I smile and feather our lips together. I won't need to punish her to elicit the effect I desire. I know my hands and hips are pressing into bone-deep bruises, and I squeeze a little harder before sliding off to her side.

Kissing her deeper, taking her lower lip between mine, I trace down her chin with my middle finger. I don't press hard, just smoothly glide over her skin down to her collarbone. I walk two fingers lightly across this ridge, and she gasps inside my mouth. Her chest is a tortoise shell of black and blue that starts at this ridge and ends below her breasts.

I continue sucking her mouth into mine, biting her tongue when she gasps louder from a squeeze to each nipple. It's almost as sweet as the first moan she gave me on our honeymoon night.

Opening the door to our hotel suite, I let Gillian walk ahead of me. She's elegant in all white; it always suits her: angelic and clean. Moving my eyes up from her graceful hips though, I'm reminded that she's not been an angel. Her back looks innocent enough under smooth white silk, but she wears the mark of another man.

"Stop." Gillian halts her walk to the sofa immediately and starts to turn towards me. "No. Stay just as you are." Her hands are still holding up the simple white rose bouquet the wedding chapel had handed to her.

She looked like purity and love walking down the aisle to me this evening. She said her vows with hardly a shake to her sweet voice. She smiled right before our lips met as man and wife. I could almost believe that she was relieved to be back in my arms.

I'm not a fool though. She stayed away. Three long years, Gillian kept herself from me.

I'm inches from her back before I even realize what I intend to do. Grabbing the neck of her dress through her mass of hair, I yank hard, feeling the rip of seams and curls along with a snarl from somewhere deep in my throat.

She screams and staggers, dropping rose petals and finally the full bouquet to the floor, narrowly stopping herself from falling forward with tiny steps. She turns with wild fear on her face. I love seeing it. "Take it off."

Shaking, she pushes the ruined dress to her feet, stepping out of it on tottering spiky heels. She looks lovely in all white lace, not much covered or left to the imagination. I smile; my bride cringes.

"That's better." I breathe a little deeper, calming and forcing myself to relax in order to enjoy tonight. I've waited long enough, no need to rush. "Sit, wife." Her body obeys with tiny jerks that start to twist her around the sofa again. "No. Don't turn your back to me." She freezes. Hands out to her sides, she's the picture of a woman trying desperately to do exactly as she's told. Perfect. "If I see, Gilli, if I see what you've done to yourself, you'll be one very sorry girl tonight. You stay facing me." She nods and finishes her little jerking dance to sit but keeps her breasts towards me.

I walk over to the set of champagne glasses and a chilled bottle on the table. A feast of snacks and desserts is laid out for us as well, but I ignore it. My appetite won't be quenched with food or drink tonight.

Filling two glasses, I walk back to stand over Gillian. She takes a glass with a small smile and thanks. "Cheers, my love, to our happy ever after." I tower over her, sipping and encouraging her to finish her glass.

With one hand, I unzip my pants. "Still thirsty?" Her wide-eyed, blinking look up morphs from confusion into submission quickly. She nods, reaching with unsteady hands to pull my cock free, as she slides herself forward on the sofa more.

I always loved getting a blowjob from her while standing. Something about looking down and only seeing peaks of her pale flesh shrouded by her thick hair always made me harder. Tonight is no exception. "Deeper, Gilli." Her little gagging sounds shoot straight to my balls, and I gently press the back of her head into me further while coming deeply down her throat. I don't release her right away; the spasms of her trying to swallow around me feel too good. A stronger retching sound finally has me stepping back.

Gillian hunches over, gasping and coughing, while tears the size of spring raindrops fall to splash on her knees. I give her a minute to compose herself, getting us each another glass.

Watching her slowly sit up more as she holds her arms around her tiny waist and brushes tears away with the heels of her palms, I have such a drowsy, euphoric thought. This is marital bliss. This is what I've been missing.

"Come here." Without looking at me, she obeys but stops a step away from me. I put my glass on the table, cross my arms, and examine her more closely. I know every tiny freckle and scar on her. There isn't a single patch of her skin that I haven't touched before. Yet, she stands before me as a mystery now. Gillian let time make her a stranger to me.

The familiar burn of rage lowers from my chest into my cock. "Take everything off." She jumps at my command, even though it was spoken quietly, calmly. She's not such a stranger after all. She responds, as she ever did, to my changing moods.

I think of all the times I had imagined having her here like this again. I picture the slow agony I had envisioned giving her at the end of my whip. I've had three years to conceive many scenarios for our reunion, each a more elaborate form of punishment and vengeance than the last. I never anticipated how overwhelming my rage would feel though.

Before she can stand upright from lowering her panties, my fist makes contact with her left shoulder. She pinwheels backwards, falling hard to the floor and sliding along the rug. As she tries to curl her body protectively inward, my foot drives into her thigh, sending her twisting to her other side. I don't give her time to recover or even move; I'm on one knee and my hands are on her.

One fist in her hair yanks her face to me; one tight grasp of both her wrists forces the rest of her to turn. There are no words, save her whimpered pleas. All the accusations I had imagined slinging at her are lost to the sea of my boiling rage.

I let go of her hair. In one quick movement, I pull my belt free and have her hands secured with it. She hardly fights me, but I know she takes being tied down as a sign of how much she's displeased me. Many times before, I've used this invaluable insight I learned from her mother to my advantage.

Gillian's cries increase with the twist of the leather against her skin as I push her hands tight against her chest.

Straddling her prone body, I like how she squeezes more tears and pleas out for me; her body bounces with them.

I'm snapped back from the abyss of rage at seeing her so helpless, so familiar, under me. Time seems to stand still as I watch her try to catch her breath and slow her crying. She keeps her eyes closed tight though.

I've hit Gillian before but only in her stomach or thighs. It's always been with the same controlled amount of force I used tonight. I brush my thumb across her shoulder, over the knot of swelling discoloration. Her mouth opens, and the sweetest gasp of pain floats out for me. "Open your eyes."

She slowly blinks; tears held back by lashes fall fast, running into her hair. I lean forward and bring our lips together for a light kiss, pressing her shoulder harder and breathing in her next deeper moan.

I know all of my imaginings were a fool's game because I never could have pictured how perfect we would be in this moment. Gillian belongs completely to me, and I'll prove it to us both.

With a deep sigh that flows into her open lips, I pull back and do what I've waited so long to do, even if I never imagined it. I punch my beautiful wife right across her cheek.

After an appropriate moment of silence for something this momentous, her scream fills the room. She writhes under me, trying to move her arms and shield her face. She wiggles to shrink away, as though she could fall through the floor and escape. I let her move a little, grinding my cock in *sync with the dance of her body. When I don't let up and don't hit her again, she finally stills, exhausted.*

Her cheek is now inflamed to match her shoulder; her whole face is a mottled mess of red and tears. She's gorgeous. "Open your eyes, wife." I'm teasing and tempting now; the rage is switched to a more controllable level of malice: one I'm familiar toying with, one I enjoy taking out on her. She's slower to obey this time, but obey she does.

I smile and wait for her to do what I know she will. She finally frowns, but her lips automatically go up in an attempt to smile too. "This is a fresh start, Gilli. You want that, don't you?" She nods, only the frown still in place now with more tears pooling up beautifully. I pull her arms above her head, almost gently pressing them against the rug. "You want to please me, don't you? You'll do whatever you can to please me from now on, won't you?" Her nods increase. "Then keep your hands above your head while I beat you." I let go of the belt and move slowly to sit up straighter, putting more of my weight on her hips. Gillian, ever the obedient girl that I helped raise, keeps her hands up.

I was reminded, on that first night as man and wife, of something that I've always known about Gillian and about myself with her. I know she doesn't enjoy pain. I won't let her be the part of herself that does because I don't *want* her to enjoy what I do to her.

Besides, it's not my Gillian's body that gives her release; it's her mind that welcomes the opportunity to please. She can't help but give in to her desire to do anything for me, anything I want. And I know that we'll be very happy together like this. She just needs to learn a few more lessons in what I expect from her, and I need to be able to trust that she won't betray me again, that she won't allow any part of herself to betray me in the future.

I pull back. My hand gently cups her right breast, my pale fingers cool against the warmth of her colored flesh. I think she surprised herself that first night of our reunion, though, with how enthusiastically she was able to climax for me, even as I choked the air from her lungs. I wasn't surprised at all. I know that she doesn't need to enjoy what I do to her to take it or to be aroused by it. That was something Anya never could understand.

I lean back, arms behind my head against the padded headboard. "Take my pants off, Gilli."

She's quick to obey, despite the wincing she does at moving. I watch her fingers delicately work, untying my sleep pants and gently pulling them down and off. She folds them neatly and puts them on the bench at the end of the bed. I don't let her return to me. "Stop. Crawl on top of me from there. Slowly."

Her knees are a little red from being pulled across the carpet two days ago, but she doesn't hesitate to get on them now. Her nipples stand up as her breasts gently move, the color on her chest darker from this angle; her hips sway, a little exaggerated for me as she knows I like.

She can't hold in a small cry as her pussy positions perfectly over me, but she tries. I think she believes holding in her sounds of suffering will hold off my excitement at hearing them. A ridiculous thought, but I do enjoy knowing that she's trying to not fuel my desire to hurt her more. It makes doing it that much more pleasurable for me really.

I smile widely for her. "Put me inside you, my love. I need to feel you around me." She takes a deep breath and pinches her lower lip with her teeth. She tries to go slow, attempting to brace herself against the onslaught of pain. I watch her face contort with the effort.

I wait until she has half of me in her, then grab her hips and dig my fingers into flesh that already wears purpled outlines of my prints. I slam the rest of the way deep inside her. Her cry out is loud and shakes her body nicely on top of me. Her eyes squeeze closed, and her head lifts back with another sob.

"Open your eyes. I want to watch you cry for me." I continue pulling her up slowly and forcing her down quickly. She gives me her tears freely, and I time my thrusts to get the most out of her low, continuous moans of pain. I know she's almost numb with it, but it makes it hard to hold back for long, feeling how swollen and tight she is from my abuse.

I let go of one hip, and she knows to keep riding me as I guide her forward with each dip onto me, pushing her faster. I run my right hand up her stomach, between her bouncing breasts, to clutch her throat.

Her eyes plead, but her voice is strangled and flat. "Please."

"Please what, my love?" I'm getting out of breath with holding back. I squeeze my fingers on her hip and throat more. "Please choke you so you can come hard for me like you did last night?" I know this isn't what she means; her whole body tries to tell me no. "Say it."

She attempts to swallow against my hand but can't. I watch her fight the urge to bring her hands off my chest to try and pull my hand away. I only smile, slamming into her more. "Say it, or you'll be in your room with a plug up your bottom all day."

Her tears make it hard to understand her, but she finally gets it out as I feel myself throb, emptying deep inside her. I watch her shudder and sob through her own release, squeezing me tighter than I thought she could.

I help her body slowly fall onto my chest and hold her against me, not letting her up until her tears are all spent. "That's my good girl, my sweet Gilli girl." I push her hair away and wipe her tears, tasting my fingers.

Her voice is raw and a whisper still edged with sobs. "Did I please you, Miles?"

"Yes. Very much." I gently lift her off and roll with her to the side. Pushing her hair away again, I kiss her bottom lip gently. "Take a quick shower. I'll get us breakfast. You've earned having it here with me this morning." She smiles at my gift.

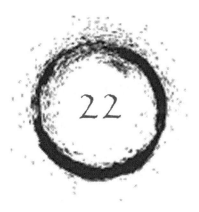

Seattle: Grace/Gillian

The click of the door, it cuts my days in half. Click starts my endless hours of painful loneliness and introspection by day. Click starts my endless hours of painful submission and coercion by night. By day, by night, this has gone on for weeks on end.

Today is supposed to be my last day, but Miles has threatened further punishment too. I don't doubt that he would prolong my solitary confinement in this room. I have no idea what he has planned really. I can only hope that he'll let me out of here tonight and not bring me back in the morning.

I know that the best way to make that happen is to appease him. Lying in here quietly, day after day, it's all I can do right now. Maybe he'll soften; maybe he'll be gentler if he thinks he can trust in my submission again. Maybe he won't lock me in here for another day…

Hello?

I only hear a dull echo against the stage floor and looming darkness to my plea for the others to break my solace. Funny, the stage always seemed a brighter place before these weeks of isolation. Perhaps it was because I felt the presence of the others more, or because I lived on the stage more than out here. I don't know, but it adds to my loneliness now.

As crazy as it sounds, I miss Miles when I'm in here.

This room is too Spartan with its one single bed, scratchy linens and blanket. There's one bare-bones bathroom with no walls for privacy and no mirror to reflect what Miles has done to me either. But I've found that if I fill up the sink and let the water get very still, holding my breath and my hair back, I can just make out a reflection. I can just see the swelling and discoloring.

Miles never touched my face before as punishment. I worry what it means that he does now. Is he no longer afraid of being questioned? Is he so certain in his position that he doesn't fear any accusations about abuse? Or is this a line in the sand? A demarcation of before and after, a way of showing how very different things will be between us? He's no longer bound by Mother's rules; that much is clear by my watery reflection.

I turn back to the rest of the room. Hard, dark surfaces greet me. Floor, wall, ceiling and bed, all an indistinguishable muddy brown. There's no natural light, just one tiny exposed bulb that I have no control over. It does nothing to push the walls out, only provides a dim view of my claustrophobic quarters.

There are also four cameras, one for each corner, all perfectly aimed and always on. I can hear their small buzz in the silence of the room. There's nothing else to hear except my breathing. Not even a sliver of light shines through from the hallway outside this door. I know no sound escapes from either side.

I'm supposed to stay here, not go to the stage. I'm not allowed to withdraw. Miles has made it abundantly clear what will happen if I let one of the others take my place. I wouldn't want Baby, Lilly or Jill to suffer in here anyway. It's too cold and dark for them, and I haven't seen or heard from Gigi in these weeks.

But I know that if I lie on the bed and curl up with my face to the pillow, I can pretend to sleep. I can go inside, step one foot onto the stage for a little while at least, and seek solace with the others while still staying ready on the outside.

It's all I have to hold on to for now. It's all that keeps me sane during this time. I don't know how much longer I can stay out, away from the comfort of the stage. I don't think I can take another day in here by myself, or another night out there with Miles.

Am I still sane?

I ask the empty stage, but it's really a question I ask myself yet again.

It's been three weeks, and I've not just submitted to Miles' punishments and demands, I've given myself to him completely, just as I did before.

Even now, curled on this bed, my fingers move down between my clenched legs to find my sore sex. I've taken everything that Miles has done, endured the pain just as he wants. Just thinking about submitting to him, I find myself aroused and willing. I don't like his painful punishments; I'm not like Gigi. I don't get turned on by pain and violence, but I still find myself willingly giving in to him. I still long for the moments when I know I've truly pleased him, no matter the cost.

I should be ashamed. How could I think about him and be excited? How could I want to please him? After all that he's done!

Should I be...ashamed?

With no answer, my thoughts go to Simon as they have every day in here. I hang on to moments I had with him, keeping those memories alive and with me. I can't help but compare Simon to Miles. I know our body has experienced other men, consensually and not, but I've only known two lovers.

Simon was gentle and demanding. I feel myself getting hotter just thinking of his kisses. Best not to think of what else his mouth could do, I think with a smile secreted by the pillow. Those thoughts only end in frustration. I wouldn't dare try to relieve myself for fear of what Miles would think. I move my hand to rest back on the pillow, next to my face. Miles has the live feed from the cameras sent to him. Every night, he questions me about my time spent in here.

That thought makes me feel less lonely somehow, knowing Miles is watching me…

Surely, my sanity is slipping, and I should be ashamed…

Still, there's no answer.

My thoughts run back to Simon. It's a small solace while I'm imprisoned here, knowing that he's free and I gave him that. It doesn't matter that he doesn't know of my gift. He gave me so much; I don't mind if he thinks the scales are tipped.

Simon was honest and raw. I felt safe in his arms. He didn't hold back, and he was unpredictable, but I always knew that he wouldn't deceive me. Simon wouldn't hurt me either. True, he threatened to put Gigi in a cave and torture her, but she would've liked that, I'm sure.

I giggle with that thought. It's a strange sound in this room and one I quickly stifle for fear of what it will look like on camera. With a deep sigh, I roll into the pillow more, moving my hand back to between my legs. Thoughts of Simon are painful; thoughts of sex with him are torturous.

But I just can't help myself. I need to be distracted from all the fear, isolation, and…and boredom. I've never spent this much time all by myself before. I don't like it at all.

A clear image of Simon comes to my mind. It was a day we spent together in bed, well, mostly together. I shared him with the others a little. I shared him with Gigi more than I wanted…

I shrug that thought away and focus on the thought of Simon again. His mouth was on me, right where my finger is currently touching. Simon had the most amazing tongue. It was…muscular. I giggle again and turn it into a cough for the cameras, bringing my hands up to cover my mouth.

When I'm calmer, when I think it's safe again, I return my fingers to the place Simon loved to touch. He spent a whole half hour I think, playing with me once, a finger at a time, seeing which one made me moan the loudest. It was his ring finger that had the perfect…pressure and angle. My clit was overly sensitive by then, but Simon waited to explore inside my lips. He waited until my moaning was more than I could take. I begged for his fingers inside me, anything inside me, before he finally slipped in just the one ring finger. Alone in my cell, I moan as long as I did that day for Simon. I can practically feel him here with me.

I pop my eyes open, flattening myself to the hard bed, guiltily not moving my hands at all. I let out one long, soundless breath, slowly bringing my hands away.

Thoughts of Simon are no use to me. I have to think of Miles now. That's what he would want. It's what will get me out of here; it's what will save me. A tear chokes my throat as I have the same thought that has also plagued me in here…Simon didn't love only me as Miles does. I know Gigi had his heart too…

Grace?

Lilly! Oh, thank goodness...I thought I'd be here all alone today.

Tears of relief soak into the pillow. I can't leave the physical sensations behind completely, or I might give too much evidence that I'm disobeying Miles' rule. I keep my feet firmly straddled between this room and the stage and feel everything on both sides.

I'm here. So is Jill. Are you...has Miles hurt you badly?

I'm all right.

The pain is everywhere, but in these hours alone at least, I can withdraw from it as long as I remember to act in pain for the cameras. It's not difficult to pretend the shuffling steps and stooped shoulders that accompany the all too real pain when I'm out of this room.

Would you like me to come out? I'll stay still and quiet...Miles won't know, I promise.

That's sweet, Lilly. Just having you stay with me is enough. We can't risk doing anything to anger Miles. He promised this will be the last day in here.

He didn't promise exactly, but I know we both need the hope. His threat of keeping us in here is enough to ensure my obedience. I've thought of running, of course. I've had a few moments to myself these few weeks, but I know running right now would be foolish. I wouldn't even get down the long drive before I would be hauled back here and in worse trouble. He would surely take his anger out on Simon too then.

Am I a fool? Even with all that's happened, I don't regret coming here willingly. It was the only way to make sure that Miles wouldn't punish Simon because of me.

You're not a fool, Grace. You're the bravest girl I know.

I didn't realize I'd asked the question to her. My mind breaks up in here. It's too similar to what Mother used to do when I was a little girl. I shudder in the cold with the hint of those memories, of being locked up for hours.

I'm not like Lilly and Gigi. I don't remember every detail of my life. My memories are clouded and never linger. The doctors said it was my ability to compartmentalize my feelings and thoughts that allowed me to accept so much of what happened in my past, not that they really knew our past. Even with Mother gone, Miles didn't want us telling details. I don't know what he thought those doctors could really do if we couldn't confide anything to them, but we wouldn't have shared with strangers anyway, even without his warning.

I think the doctors may have been right though. My painful memories sift through me like sand through stretched fingers. Only small pieces cling and stay around for me to keep; the rest just disappear. I know not where, and I don't care.

It makes living through these weeks of isolation and punishment bearable. Even with being forced to experience all the pain that accompanies the nights with Miles, only my body retains the mark of each blow. I've already forgotten most of what happened on our honeymoon night.

That doesn't make me brave, only lucky I think.

Thank you, Lilly. I only meant that I haven't thought about escaping.

What would be the point? Jill and I have talked for hours, coming up with all sorts of plans, but until you can walk around freely...what's the point?

I sigh with her straight-forward logic. I want to tell her that it's not the question of whether or not there's a possibility of escape, but the fact that I've not planned one on my own that has me feeling a fool and questioning what's wrong with me. I could talk to Gigi about this; she wouldn't empathize with me, but I wouldn't have to explain it to her either. Lilly's too young to understand my self-doubts.

Have you seen Gigi?

Lilly only shakes her head in response.

Sighing into the pillow, I turn over and stare up at the brown ceiling. But Lilly's voice has me face down in the pillow again to hide my reaction, an excitement at a possible distraction. Anything is better than more brown emptiness.

I think you should know what she's up to though. Gigi got rid of the others.

What do you mean? What others?

You know...the ones we never see, but we can hear crying or screaming sometimes.

I shudder and hold myself in the same manner as Lilly. Terrible sounds come from the dark corners beyond the light of the stage.

How did she get rid of them?

Lilly only shrugs in reply before adding, *I only know that they're gone. See for yourself.*

I risk stepping fully inside and walk to the edge of the stage. What was only darkness before is now lighter. No, it's not light but illuminated somehow. It reminds me of the night sky when the moon isn't full and stars so far away seem brighter. The silence is like being under water; every sound is muffled and carried away to limitless depths.

I retreat back out quickly, but a thought occurs to me in a panic, *Where's Baby?*

Lilly shrugs again but doesn't add what we both think now. Gigi wouldn't have gotten rid of Baby, would she? She couldn't, could she?

We're silent for so long, I almost fall asleep in the emptiness of this room. Lilly's voice is shy and quiet when she speaks again. *Would you like me to tell you your horoscope, Grace?*

I feel a smile spread across my lips. I know she has countless charts and readings memorized. I think she could predict our days for each of us for another millennium without ever having to consult her computer program and books.

Yes, please.

Lilly clears her throat before starting in her most studious, professional voice, *Saturn is in Scorpio now, so you'll have a grave struggle to gain control over your own circumstances. But there is an end in sight with a full moon lunar eclipse signifying closure. Even this is complicated, though, with a hard angle to Pluto and Uranus. This means you should expect the unexpected, Grace, but hold on to the hope the full moon promises still.*

It's not as hopeful as I want, but an end in sight is something. Hearing Lilly talk about horoscopes and future plans for escape is nice. I can convince myself that she's right. Nothing is so bad today. We'll be free again tomorrow. I've convinced myself of more with a lot less to go on.

I've been able to take all that Miles has done before. I can take it still, even without Gigi's help at taking the pain. I can give myself to him, even as I fear what he will do next. I've done this before, and I can do it again. What choice is there but the one I've already made to come back here?

As long as I don't have to stay in this tiny room, I'll be all right. Miles' anger will end as it has before. I have Lilly's promise of the full moon.

I can bend my mind and body to be what Miles wants, what he needs. Even if I never escape, I can be happy with that. I can get what I need out of what Miles offers. It isn't the love I had with Simon, but Miles does love me. Doesn't he? He did choose me, and that's something...

Thank you, Lilly. I will hold on. You should check on Jill now...I can tell she's very upset.

She wants to destroy your cell. She thinks she could break the door down if she uses part of the bed...

I'm sure she could. Tell her when the time is right, I'm sure she'll be strong for all of us.

I'll wait until Miles comes in to leave.

Thank you.

I can see Lilly sitting cross-legged in the light, her fingers twisting and turning in puzzles interlocked. I can just barely see Jill in the start of the shadows with her hands stuffed in her pockets and her lanky hair pulled down in front to further hide her features.

I close my eyes to blot out the brownness of this room, my cell.

And I force myself to not think of Gigi, Baby, Simon or even Miles. I force myself to sleep and think of waking free from here and strong enough to take what will come next, whatever that may be.

My dreams walk me along a beach in a full moon. I can almost feel the sand shifting and memories fading in the pale light.

The Stage: Red/Gigi

The landscape is changing again. I stumble a little as my feet push piles of sand forward with each step. My path is now a steady incline. I finally reach the top of a dune and have a vantage point to see where I'm heading. I snort a chuckle. See isn't exactly the right word. I know that I'm not really seeing any of this, but it helps to ground me to think of myself as the one constant in here, a self with gravity and senses.

A bigger laugh escapes me, echoing off sand and sky and wispy grasses, all the nonexistent things I can't really see but do anyway. The stage allows for all sorts of unimaginable imaginings. This one, a beach with no water, is becoming familiar to me.

I've been drawn to it, as if pulled by a giant magnet, yet it's stayed just beyond my footsteps before now. Each time I felt a sandy grit to a wind that doesn't really blow into my face, the image receded further away.

For what feels like an eternity, I've been traipsing through all the terrain of the stage, finding the Unknown Ones. That's what I've chosen to call them. It was important to me to give them a name since so many didn't have one.

What started off as a journey deeper into the darkness just beyond the stage's light has become a safari. Except, with each encounter of the rare creatures here, I've gained more than just a trophy souvenir. The Unknown have given themselves up to me, one by one and group by group.

I've taken their memories and experiences to be my own. It's not as an overlapping layer of paints that creates a new image or even as an overlaying of bricks that builds something new. It's not even as a puzzle with pieces fit together. It's all of these and none of them.

I'd met some of the Unknowns before, seeking them out in corners just darker than the edge of the stage when I needed to heighten a feeling with pain. I would reach my fingers, floating phantom white against the fog of blackness, out toward an Unknown, and I would *feel* so much more. It's the only word I have to describe what took place then. I didn't see; I only felt. I didn't touch; I only felt. I didn't know; I only felt.

Now, I see, I touch, I know. I am. They are a part of me now.

I feel nonexistent tears line my face, hot in this stinging wind. The doctors had called it merging of identities. That's not what it is. Merging implies that both parts are left intact, like paint that dries, brick that settles, or pieces that click. No, all that is left is me, and it's a me filled with what wasn't mine before.

I'm a thief. That's closer to what it is. I've taken what wasn't mine but was offered freely for the taking. At my nonexistent touch, an Unknown is known no more. In the end, they all cease to exist, and I am filled.

Sometimes, I find them in a group, like a herd of zebras, using their similarities to defend against the fear and blend together; usually they are all about the same age. The group I just met was like this. They were all 8 and had their arms in slings from when Anya pushed us down the basement stairs. Every time our mother used that healing arm to instill a new pain, a new girl appeared among the others. The herd stopped growing in members when the sling finally came off. I stole thirteen Unknowns' memories from that time.

It's the ones that I've met that are all alone, though, that have been the hardest for me to steal. Their memories are the strongest, even if they only encompass the tiniest sliver of a moment from our past.

I absently scratch at an itch on my right arm as I continue along the sandy ridge. This patch of wind-blown waves that shift sandy peaks into undulating hills is our ground zero. I've been hunting for this particular Unknown since I started on this safari. She is the one I knew I had to find or fail in my plan. And at last, I have her in my nonexistent sight.

My steps become easier, sliding down the slope side of this latest dune. I end with a run on hard-packed sand that has me winded. I've given up thinking about the absurdity of reality in here. I've given up thinking how crazy it is that the balls of my feet hurt from impact while I run. This is real, or it was at one time.

I pant with my hands on my knees when I finally come to a stop just outside a bordered square of sand. She sits alone inside the center of the sandbox, tiny fingers playing with clumps before dumping them on her dimpled knees. She ignores me. I always have to make the first move with the Unknowns. It looks like this time she isn't going to disappear though. My search is at an end.

I take a deep breath before slowly moving closer to her. An unfamiliar ill comes over me; I'm afraid. This one is going to hurt, and not the good kind.

"Hello, Gillian." My voice is whipped around with the wind, cut off to a dull thud when I take the extra step to stand inside the sandbox. In here, there is no wind, no sound, just a vacuum void of anything except the raspy breathing of a tiny girl.

I squat down to be at her level. She's been crying. Her cherub cheeks are streaked with tears, long dried. Sand clings to her lashes. I see more in her dark ringlets and almost reach to feather her hair away from her sweat-soaked forehead. My hand stops part way and shakes.

Pain is a palpable wave coming off her. I sink forward to my knees, a dizziness making me want to crawl away.

Get a grip! Just take her hand and be done with it all ready.

Except I don't know if that will work this time. She's the first of us, the original split from outside to inside. At least, I think she is.

Displacing sand with my knees, I push forward to be even closer. She's a tiny child, still in diapers, but that doesn't matter in here. "Gillian, do you know who I am?"

She drops the balled-up sand from her little fists and turns her face up to mine. Big, brown eyes stare with more intelligence than any tiny tot would ever possess in reality. Sand-caked fingers shoot up towards my face, and I have one moment of panic. This is *my* end. She'll take me.

Seriously. Get a grip. This is the only plan I have. I'll do what I've always done and see it to the end. I lean forward and her sharp nails gouge into my cheek. I don't pull away. I brace myself for the onslaught of her memories, closing my eyes to take them.

None come. Nothing happens. I open my eyes as she squeezes my cheek.

Why isn't this working? I reach up and take her hand to hold in both of mine, staring into her eerily cognizant eyes.

I do the only thing I can think of. "Please." I have a flash of memory, like one of those subliminal messages that skates by so quickly. There's a glimpse of red, a note of something foul, a hint of pain, but nothing more. I huff out a sigh of impatience.

I can't leave her behind. For my plan to work, I need to empty the stage of all the Unknowns. I put off thinking about Lilly and Jill. I know I'll have to go back for them too, but only if I can take this one. I had thought that Baby might've been the original, but she wasn't. This close to the child in the sand, I know I'm not wrong this time.

I try again, a little more forcefully, "Please. I need your help."

She closes her eyes, and I feel the familiar liquefying sensation start at my fingertips, a swirling of what is me and what is her. I close my eyes too, and the swirl drains us into her memories.

Our throat hurts from a tempest-sized tantrum a moment ago. The sandbox is now in its proper place, surrounded by the park near our first home. We're all alone. The glimpse of red comes into focus, Anya's lips painted into a bright grimace. Her words are hot and sharp, like her nails, talon points that she squeezes into our tiny shoulders to get a tighter grip for all the shaking she's giving us.

The world stops moving as suddenly as it had started. Fresh tears climb up and out. Anya's voice cuts through them, seething out at us with promised venom. The foul smell wafts up stronger as we're flipped over, face to sand; we choke on the grit that coated our tongue before we could close our mouth.

Baby arms push us up enough to breathe. A light breeze puts more of the disgusting smell into the air as our diaper is pushed to the side. Something foreign, hard, plastic, small, still so big, this thing is shoved inside our filthy diaper. Inside us. Our wail is snapped in half as we're in the air again, righted back to sitting with this…thing. The talons let go, and we're free to let the tempest loose again. Our screams are unending. We have a blurry view of the red walking away.

The swirling wavers and warps; the memory comes to a stop. I take a deep breath. Pain and fear linger, from both watching a horror and living through it. I breathe once more deeply, a little easier. I had my doubts that I would be the one left sitting here this time. Yet I'm still me, and I was her.

I slowly open my eyes. Gillian's wet lashes flutter on her flushed cheeks. Our hands are still linked. What the hell? I don't need to look around to know we're still in the park, alone. She didn't go away like all the others did, and we're both still trapped in her memory. But it's my memory now too.

With all the others, I felt a strength when it was over. I'd conquered the past demon and could move on. I made it what it was, a distant memory that we survived, nothing more, nothing less.

This is more. I can't stay trapped here! I pull my hand away with a sudden jerk, hoping to break the spell of whatever this is. I stay trapped next to this little girl, and I know she's still in pain. I can *feel* it inside myself.

I look around in a frenzy, with the insane thought of trying to find Anya to save me, her, us. Who walks away from a baby in a sandbox and…! My panic is too great to fill in the blank of what else we are suffering here at that evil woman's hands. I start to sob uncontrollably. Gillian moves away from me; her little chubby-ringed legs crawl a few feet to the edge of sand and grass. I close my eyes and give in to the deepest despair I've ever known. Gillian's fresh cries work in unison with mine.

I almost don't hear the sweet cooing from above us. My latest sob hitches in my throat, just as Gillian's does. I open my eyes, ridiculously hopeful that Anya has returned to rescue us, to fix what she has done. Baby arms go in the air as I lift my eyes up to see the woman standing near us.

I'd recognize her anywhere. It's Grace. In my shock, I look her up and down carefully. No. This is a woman from our past, the one Grace sees when she looks in a mirror. This woman has the same deep caramel skin as Grace, but her voice is off; it's more deep south like Jill's. Other than that, she could be Grace. Her lips are the same plump pinkness, and her same jet eyes, just above the same smattering of deeper chocolate freckles, look down with such pity and concern at the balling child at her feet.

She lifts Gillian up into her arms, planting kisses and soft hands on a scrunched, red face. Shushing noises and soft, tinkling words work to soothe us both. I blink in disbelief, trying to work out what is now, what is remembered, and who is who.

The woman carries Gillian over to a park bench, next to an elaborate stroller. I stay behind, watching as she efficiently clucks and coos through changing our messed diaper for a fresh one from the stroller. She scowls at the plastic piece of toy that we'd managed to dislodge. She deposits it with the rest of the mess into a bag, frowning and shaking her head. Her face is back to angelic serenity when she smiles down on the now softly crying child.

She lifts Gillian in a warm embrace, rocking and lulling, one hand going out to push pull the stroller in a similar rhythm. I get up to move closer to them, drawn by her sweetness. I want my own tears to be swept away by her gentle touch. The smell of roses meets me with each movement of her perfumed arm.

I sit behind her, not daring to speak or hardly breathe. This is the calmest I've ever felt on the stage, perhaps in my life. I don't want this memory to end or to start over.

Anya's voice, indignant and alarmed, comes from the other side of the sandbox. She stands with hands on hips, rage on face, and new diaper dangling from talons. She's frightening in her beauty. Insanity looks out from her dark eyes.

The woman is unfazed and stays sitting, bouncing Gillian on her knee. Anya is forced to come closer, and a new steel grip of fear binds my stomach as her face transforms to the caring and kind mask she usually only reserves for men.

Just as Anya's arms reach down to take back what is hers, Gillian puts a pudgy hand out to me. I grasp it with both of mine. The same liquid joining of us has my eyes looking back at myself. Between us, this angel, this woman, this savior gives us one last kiss on our head. Her full lips brush us with a few words, a prayer for heavenly grace to watch over us. This is what love feels like.

I close my eyes against the most tranquil tears I've ever shed. This time, I don't need to open them to know that I'm alone on a shifting sand dune. I sob loudly, uncontrolled, and with a release for all the memories that I've had to bear and for all the rest that I will have to take on.

With a final sob, a last intake of hot air, I rest. I'm alone in the silence for only a moment.

The cyclone of sand forming around me isn't a surprise. Eyes still closed, I get up to my knees, stretching my hands out high above my head. The thousands of Unknowns left out in the darkest reaches of the stage all come to me. We join hands as one, with fleeting fingers and trails of memories. I'm broken down into multiple liquid bubbles, each piece bouncing in many directions at once. I'm bombarded by all the thoughts, feelings, and actions of a thousand lifetimes, all spent in increments of singular moments.

When the sands finally stop, when the memories halt, when the bubbles come together again, I hear the faintest sound of softly lapping waves in the distance.

I open my eyes and stand, free and not quite as unbound. And I'm still me.

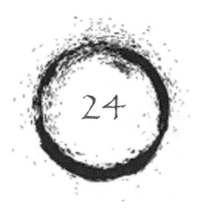

Seattle: Miles Vanderson

Watching Gillian sleep, I can almost forget the pain she's caused me. I can almost forget how she ripped open my heart with leaving me. I can almost pretend that I wasn't in hell for three years because of her.

But that's over now. We are getting our fresh start, and I need to put our past behind us once and for all.

I brush a stray strand away from her face, but her breathing stays deep; her eyes stay in motion behind tightly squeezed lids. Does she dream of me? I'd like to think so, but I won't ask. I'd know if she lied, and I don't want to know if she dreams of Lamb.

I kneel next to my bed, *our* bed. Gillian is *my* wife, and this is *our* marital bed. These simple thoughts give me such joy that I can truly forget all about the pain, almost.

No one can come between us ever again. She'll learn that today, if she doesn't already know it.

With my fingers flat on the bed, barely touching her arm, her tiny whimper halts my waking her. She shudders and twists towards me a little before settling back in peace, a smile spreading with her lips and legs.

I smile too, knowing now that she does dream of me, of last night. I brought her here from her room, and she showed her gratitude for being released finally from her three week imprisonment. She understands that any disobedience of my rules will result in her quick return.

I know the threat of that room isn't enough though. Inside my sweet girl lurks another who isn't so easily controlled, one not so obedient.

I discussed that very topic with Anya only a few days before she died, but she wasn't interested in my theories of how best to help her daughter then. She had her own ideas on the subject.

"We're taking a risk, meeting like this." I don't stop fingering Anya's open slit.

"Nonsense. Martin is a sound sleeper, and the sleeping pill I added to his nightly brandy did the trick early tonight."

Her fingers stroke me with a lazy and familiar touch, my length hardening as I remember Gillian's mouth from this afternoon.

"We should awaken Gilli."

Anya twists under the fur throw, her face inflamed by more than the fire from the library hearth, but she quickly reassembles her features to her usual, more provocative look. She's beautiful, like her daughter, but there's more guile to her than Gillian could ever evoke. "We don't need her to have our fun, not tonight, Miles." Her fingers trace over my stomach and back down. "Besides, I could see how frustrated you were with her this afternoon, how disappointed in her you were."

It's true. I've had less patience with Gillian's craziness lately. I'm home for a few weeks now, and I hope to clear up an issue that has been troubling me.

"She seems capable of taking so much."

"Hmm." Anya lowers herself, eyes lit with a secret pleasure as she brings her mouth to my tip.

I moan with the feel of her tongue up and back down my hardened rod. She's really quite good, and Gillian's learned all her best tricks. I manage to breathe out, "I think we shouldn't allow her to enjoy her punishments so much is all."

"Hmm." Her mouth full and working, no clear words escape, but I can make out that she's saying 'who cares?'

"Because punishment shouldn't be enjoyed by the punished." I sound like a pulpit-thumper from Cotton

Mather's day. I tilt Anya's chin up; her eyes glaze with a familiar lust. "We should be the only ones that enjoy hurting her. While punished, she should learn her lesson."

She smiles. "Perhaps you're right. She's a willful little bitch." Her head lowers again to continue pleasing me.

I let her words settle the matter for a moment, twisting the curls of her silky dark hair in my fingers as I enjoy the depth of her throat against me.

Being Martin Vanderson's son has taught me one thing: I don't need to take no for an answer. "I want to force Gillian to no longer, hmm, change when we punish her." I keep the lust from my voice. I won't reveal my desire for Gillian's pain without her pleasure from it, but I know the subject of Gillian's psychological issues is touchy with Anya. She refuses to discuss it for the most part.

She sits up quickly, wiping her full lips and kneeling in front of me. "I don't see how you'd plan on making that happen." She smiles more, a sinful look made even more wicked with the fire dancing shadows over her. "Besides, I quite enjoy seeing her come at the end of your whip." She laughs and falls on top of me, covering my body with hers for a moment before swiftly repositioning herself. She has me inside her in a matter of seconds, and I groan with the fast pace her hips set.

She finally slows and leans in close against me to whisper, "I like knowing that I've made her into a hungry little slut for every painful thing we do to her."

I smile watching Gillian sleep now, her breathing even and relaxed again. Her mother may not have thought it could be done, but I had faith that my love for her was enough to bring her out of her craziness. I just need to maintain a firm grip of control over her to prevent her from lapsing into her other selves ever again. I have a perfect plan for that as well.

"Gilli, my love, time to wake up." I gently rock her arm and whisper against her forehead with a kiss. She moans and stirs before her eyes slowly open.

It takes a few blinks for her to come fully awake and to realize the painful reality of her body. But just as she has every morning for three weeks, she smiles sweetly at me, even as her brows twist with the pain of sitting up.

I can hear the small cry she breathes through. She's holding back tears as she brings her legs off the bed. I only stand back and let her move on her own, watching how stiffly she rises.

When she finally looks up again, standing unsteadily, her smile is gone. That doesn't matter this morning though. I smile enough for us both. "Breakfast is waiting, but you have time to bathe first. A hot shower will do you good."

She nods and smiles a weak thank you, moving past me towards the bathroom. "But first." She halts instantly, and I feel myself harden just as quickly. "I have something to show you and something to give you."

She turns back, and my love for her grows as much as my balls tighten at the look of abject fear in her eyes. She takes hesitant steps back to me, and I motion for her to sit down on the bed.

I take the small envelope from the nightstand and watch her look change from fear to confusion. "I'm going to ask you a question, and I know you understand that I expect your complete honesty in answering me." She nods and swallows, fear back on her lovely features. "Did you love Simon Lamb?"

I watch carefully as she starts to withdraw but quickly stops herself and refocuses. I give her the moment she needs, as I've done every night when my punishments have become more difficult for her to take. She eventually gives in to her need to please me, to submit herself to me.

This last punishment will be no different: painful for her but necessary. And it will be pleasing to me, even as I know now that I won't like her answer.

Seattle: Grace/Gillian

I start to nod but realize it wouldn't be an acceptable answer to Miles. "I thought I did." I know I loved Simon. I still do, but even in this fog of pain, I know I have to keep my wits.

I've never known Miles to be jealous. Then again, I've never given him a reason to be before. He hasn't mentioned Simon or anyone else since I've been back. I had thought that he didn't care, that so long as I was with him, nothing else mattered.

I can see how wrong I was by the calm look of rage taking over his face. I jump at the chance to stop it from becoming all-consuming. "I know I didn't feel the same for him as I do for you."

No good. The rage has settled into a smirk on his lips. "Of course not, my love. *Our* love is genuine and real. What you felt for him was but a trick." He cups my face with his free hand and gently rubs my cheek with his thumb. I try not to pull away as he presses against a bruise on my jaw. "He used your sweet nature against you. It's not your fault that you fell for his manipulations."

I can't tell if this means that he's not angry with me, only Simon. Before I can ask, he offers me the envelope with both his hands stretched out to me. I slowly reach for it, afraid of what I'll find inside. Lilly and Jill are both silently watching too. I wish Gigi were here; she would know what to say, how to act.

I hold my breath as I take out photos of Simon, numbly flipping from one to the next. I only remember to breathe again when Miles speaks, "I know this may be painful for you to see, but I need you to understand that you gave yourself to a man who had no real feelings for you. See, Gilli, Lamb's not been thinking or worrying about *you* at all." His finger drags across the photo of Simon with his cousin and several barely dressed women. It's a dark resolution, but it's still easy to see that Simon is drunk, and the women are pressed against him. "This one was taken two days ago."

When I lower the stack onto my lap, Miles lifts my wrists back up. "Go through all of them." I continue flipping, taking a moment to stare at each one since I know this is what Miles wants now. He means to rub my nose in how little I meant to Simon.

Maybe it's the pain I feel all over or only the pain this causes my heart, but I simply don't care when the tears slip from my eyes down to the glossy prints, swept away when I flip to the next image. I don't care that Miles is standing over me and watching as I mourn another man. I don't care that this makes me an even bigger idiot. I can hear Lilly cautioning me to be more stoic. I don't even answer her.

Miles finally takes the photos from me and puts them back into the envelope. I keep my head down, sniffing the last of my tears away.

I know it shouldn't matter. Gigi told Simon goodbye with that note, but *I* didn't get to tell him. Now it seems that it wouldn't have mattered to him anyway.

A part of me is glad that Simon has forgotten me so easily. Now I can forget him too. It'll make being with Miles easier if I don't have to compare him to Simon.

I already know that if we do find a way out of here, I'll never be able to go back to San Francisco. Miles would find me too easily, and he'd hurt Simon for sure then. Lilly was pretty blunt about analyzing that possibility. So, it's good that Simon doesn't want me. I'm glad that it's only *my* heart that is broken.

I lift my chin to look at Miles but stop at his lips as I always do. I close myself off from Lilly and Jill. I know Miles isn't done with me by the coldness in his smile, and it's easier to take what he does if I don't have to fight the urge to run inside and hide with them.

Seattle: Miles Vanderson

Watching her cry over the photos Spencer's man took has a strange effect on me. I expected to be angry if she reacted with any sign of being upset by Lamb's betrayal. Instead, I can feel my excitement building.

I had Spencer keep track of Lamb in case he became a problem after her disappearance. Three weeks of watching the man vacillate between misanthrope and gigolo, and I'm convinced that he's nothing to think about. Still, he had my

Gillian at his whim. And Lamb's still out there; her tears still fall for him.

I should be enraged, but the smile on my face only widens more. I can't help feeling happy, knowing that her only other experience with another man has been bleak and futile. She can't possibly pine away for long, not for a man that would forget her so quickly, and certainly not when I've shown my devotion by looking tirelessly for her for three years! I know she appreciates my love, even if part of her ran from it.

Her tears are a fitting end to the journey she started when she let herself be pulled away from me. She *should* cry over the uselessness, the very emptiness, of her leaving my love behind, even if it was another of her selves who did it. But that won't matter anymore.

I sit on the bed next to her and pull her into my arms, feeling her damp cheek through my shirt. Her soft voice is softened even more by my shoulder. "I told Simon that I belonged to another, that I couldn't belong to him." My heart flutters with her perfect words because I know she's telling me the truth. Gillian understands that she's always been mine.

"I know he hurt you, but that's behind you now." I brush her hair away and pull her to sit on my lap fully. I gently lift her chin, admiring how she manages to look angelic and calm, even with the tears still clinging to her lashes and the bruises only starting to fade. I've done a number on Gillian's face, her whole body really.

I wanted her to know that nothing is off limits from now on. I like seeing her face reflect our new understanding.

I'm not afraid to express my anger however I see fit. I don't care if the staff sees what I've done to her. I won't limit my attentions to only that which can't be seen as Anya did. Gillian will bear the humiliation of public scrutiny as well as the knowledge that I enjoy it. She's never leaving these grounds again, so it doesn't matter anyway.

"I won't ever let anyone hurt you, my love. As my wife, no man will ever have that chance again." She returns my smile, but she's still tentative. I know she expects me to punish her, and I weigh that option against my plans.

"I have something for you that will keep you safe." And mine. "Put out your hands and close your eyes." She sniffs one last time and wipes her eyes with both hands before doing as I've instructed.

She obediently keeps her eyes closed and arms out, even as I shift and jostle her a little pulling a velvet bag out of my pants pocket. I place the drawstring bag in the center of her hands. "You may open your eyes now."

She only stares at the bag, waiting for permission to do anything else. I smile at how much she's changed from three weeks ago, or even three years ago.

She was always submissive, always eager to please. Her body always gave in, even as she would withdraw or hide. Even when she allowed herself pleasure from the punishments with a false personality, her need to please was always there. Her mother taught me how to take full advantage of it. But these weeks together have brought out her deepest desires to submit to me. By not allowing her an escape, both literally and figuratively, I've forced her to face those desires. I've forced her to embrace them.

"Open it."

She pulls the tie loose and reaches in with her fingers, pulling out the glittering cuff. She looks from me to the bracelet with a small frown. "It's beautiful, Miles."

"It's yours." I take it from her and move the cuff slowly so the light can catch the diamonds on the front of the white gold band. "I had it specially made just for you." She puts her wrist out for me, but I wait to put it on.

"I know I said that a large wedding ring was garish and didn't fit your sweet beauty." She nods and looks at the simple band on her outstretched hand, a smaller match to the one on mine. "But I did want you to have something befitting a woman of your status, of *my* status." She frowns more as I continue, her wrist still out for me as though she'd forgotten it was lifted. "I wanted something that you could wear for every occasion."

She slowly responds, "It's perfect."

"Yes. It is, just like you, my love." I kiss her cheek gently. "And also just like you, this bracelet will stay put." Her frown is deeper now, as I think she starts to understand my hidden meaning. I take the bag from her and reach in for the tiny key at the bottom, opening the hidden clasp at the back of the bracelet.

I slip the cuff on her but don't close it, just turn her wrist over again to admire how it looks. The band is a perfect fit, not too wide, not too small. The circular cluster of diamonds is both simple and elegant.

"Inside this bracelet is a GPS tracking system, Gilli. I have an application on my phone and computers that will tell me where you are at all times. I can even listen to where you are and what you're doing. I can find you anywhere with this." I tap the bracelet and her wrist bounces.

I hand the key to her, and the confusion on her face is priceless. "This key will lock that bracelet in place with no chance of it coming loose, no chance of it being taken off." I wait for this to sink in; her confusion turns to a wary fear as her fingers pinch the tiny key. "I want you to lock yourself in and hand me the key." I smile, a little self-conscious at how melodramatic I sound.

"It's a symbolic gesture only, but I think it's important for you to understand that I don't expect just your placid submission. I expect your complete cooperation in giving yourself to me, in all matters. This little token of my love will ensure that even if you are unable to maintain control over yourself, there will be no running, no escaping, no hiding from me ever again."

With a thoughtful moment of hesitation, she calmly puts the key to the slip of a lock and twists it into place. She's serene and steady as she offers the key back to me on her open palm, a small smile on her lips even. "Thank you for such a beautiful gift, Miles." She puts her cool fingers to my cheek and warm lips to the other side of my face as I take the key from her.

I narrow my eyes, watching her, but she doesn't reveal any thoughts. She's not withdrawn in her usual sense, but somehow, she's not quite the same either; she's calmer.

I'm reminded of a documentary I saw years ago about long-held prisoners that have a hard time dealing with their freedom and choose to put themselves back in custody through obvious criminal activities. They feel safer, more secure, with the familiar setting behind bars and choose prison over freedom in the long run.

I smile with the thought that Gillian understands this bracelet will protect her against herself, against any foolish thoughts of freedom. She's already chosen her safer, more secure place here with me. She winces with pain as I move to put the key into my pocket again.

"I'm glad you like it so much. You'll have a chance to show it off soon." She raises her eyebrows but waits for me to continue.

She's so perfectly obedient and submissive, my heart swells with love for her. My pants do as well. They'll be time for that after breakfast.

"I'm going to throw my beautiful wife a proper homecoming party next weekend. We'll invite everyone to celebrate your return and our marriage. Would you like that, my love?"

She swings her arms around my shoulders despite the obvious pain to her back, squeezing me with a squeal of delight. "That would be wonderful, Miles! We haven't had a party here in so long."

I kiss her parted lips and take my time exploring the warmth of her mouth with my tongue for a moment before pulling back and standing her up. Looking her up and down, it's obvious that she's still quite hurt.

Keeping her from withdrawing does have its side effects; she can't ignore the various abuses I've inflicted on her like she used to do so easily. She doesn't stand fully erect now, and she favors her left side still. This won't do for a party.

"You'll have to be on your best behavior from now until then, Gilli, so I won't have to punish you so severely."

She nods and promises to not make me angry. We both know that it isn't only anger that motivates my desire to hurt her, but I smile at her sweet promise. I can wait until after the party to beat her again. Her injuries should be mostly healed by then, and a fresh palette is always inspiring to me.

I kiss her head one last time. "I told you I'll always take care of you. I love you, Gilli."

"And I love you, Miles." Something in her voice is distant. I can't read anything different in her eyes though.

"And don't worry about getting the bracelet wet. Nothing can harm it." I smile and leave her to get ready for our day together. As I close the door, she's still standing in the same spot, holding her wrist up with her other hand and staring at the bracelet.

I'll know if she tries to take it off, but that's a feature I'll keep to myself for now.

The Stage: Red/Gigi

Take the key, Grace.

Gigi?! Oh, God. Where have you been?

I'm here now, Grace.

What should I do?

Take the key and do exactly as Miles says. I have a plan. Stay calm.

But then we'll never be free!

I know. Take the key, Grace. And smile for him.

Anderson Valley: Simon Lamb

Am I a fool?

Really wish I could get that fucking thought outta my head. Rolling over, taking care not to look at my phone on the nightstand, I sit up on my bed's edge. I know it's early. I didn't lie down until almost 3:00 a.m.

And I didn't get to sleep at all.

So it's probably 4:00, maybe 4:30? Fuck. I snatch my phone up and swipe it awake. It's no use to pretend I'll sleep anyway. The lit screen puts off an eerie glow and shows me that it's only 3:30. Great. Hours to go before I can start another fucking day. Time has become my enemy.

It's been 24 days like this—24 days and Red still hasn't come back; Grace hasn't tried to reach me. My anger has been building for 24 days.

At first, I waited because I thought she'd come to her senses. Even with Red's note making it clear she didn't want to be found, I believed that deep down one of her would see the light of day and come crawling back to me. And I hadn't planned on making it easy for her when she did.

For the first week, my pride wouldn't let me think for a second that she'd *stay* away. I figured she was off licking her wounds and fuming, maybe even fucking someone else to get back at me. I briefly entertained the possibility that she might have gone off with that asshole, Miles, just to *really* get back at me.

One call to Bradford eased my mind about that at least. Seems Cary had clued him in on just how pissed off I was about the whole situation. Bradford was groveling when he swore he gave Miles a different guy to contact in the future. He also said he didn't expect Miles back in the Bay area anytime soon. It looks like I rattled the pompous prick more than I thought. In an otherwise fucked up week, there was a small amount of satisfaction in that.

In that timeframe, I let my hot anger turn cold and calculating. I enjoyed imagining all the ways I would torture Red for every minute she kept me waiting. I was wrong though; apparently she never intended to return. That only led to more anger.

And hidden behind all that anger? I feel like a fucking game show host. Well, behind curtain #1 are feelings this fucker isn't prepared to think about and an all-inclusive stay in perdition. Congratulations, contestants, thanks for playing.

I laugh at myself. After Red and Grace were a no-show, I had to face the fact that I was on unfamiliar ground with her. Again. Don't need to think about my feelings 'cause I can't get away from them now.

Guilt over how I scared her? Yep, check. Right there, every time I close my eyes, there's that look on Red's face just before she stormed off and a pit in my gut—feels like when I slammed my nuts into the base sliding for home plate when I was seven.

I can't shake the feeling of guilt over threatening her. It doesn't help that I meant it. I wasn't just *threatening* to treat her like one of my products; I was going to. Fuck Grace's softness and all the others' vulnerabilities. I wanted to drag her down into my cave and take every bit of my wrath out on her, no matter which identity showed up. It also doesn't help my conscience that I can so easily picture the look of devastation on Red's face when I demanded she switch places with Grace.

It was the hard truth of these facts that stopped me from chasing after her. My pride got in the way of me hunting her down at first, but it was this nagging fucking guilt and uncertainty that kept me from doing what comes natural to me.

That is, until last week—the supposed deadline I'd given myself to wait for her to come around. Or for me to get a fucking handle on my conscience again.

I've been living in a drunken, stoned, fucked up mess since that day, simply because I can't get past what I've thought all along.

I can't hunt her down. I can't drag her back here. I can't treat her like that. As much as every part of me wants to, I know I can't. Once I got her in the cave—once that line was crossed—I just wouldn't be able to do it.

And I'm angry with her for not belonging to me like that—completely. Like a spoiled fucking child, I've been enraged at her willingness to walk away from me. I've waited for her to return so I could keep thinking that whatever I want is good enough for her.

But she hasn't returned, and I know she won't. After all this time, 24 days, it's pretty clear she's not going to give in.

FUCK!

So who the fuck needs a fucked up chick with five fucking personalities anyway?! I should listen to Cary and get back to my old life. It was a good life.

My toes squish in the plush rug under my bed. I rub my hands against stubble and smell the hint of whiskey and pot over unbrushed teeth.

Funny thing is I've not let a single woman into my bed since Red or Grace. I've partied with plenty of sluts, usually with Cary. He's been like an ambassador showing me around Pusslandia the last few days. It's like he's on a mission to see me securely back to my old ways.

But I haven't fucked any of them. Even with a raging hard-on, I just come back here or to my apartment in the city and try to sleep—alone.

Who needs a fucked up chick with five personalities? Me, that's who. I don't want anyone else. I want Red. I want Grace. I want all of her, and I blew it. I fucking blew it, and now I've probably waited too long.

Fuck.

A sob escapes my lips, and I slurp it back through tight teeth. My nose runs and burns from too much coke and the sting of unshed tears. I've allowed myself to wallow pretty deep, I think, laughing hard at the storm of unfamiliar emotions. I know it's the combination of booze, drugs and lack of sleep that has me crying like a fucking bitch right now. But damn, it feels good to get it out for a second.

My head feels a little clearer. Crying bitch. Good thing Cary isn't here, or I'd never hear the end of it.

Without opening my eyelids, I pull blindly at the drawer of my nightstand. My fingers caress the familiar lines of hard paper, pinching the edges and pulling it out. I know below this note is my letter from Grandfather. Two people I cared about and both are gone; both left nothing more than ink on paper.

Abandonment issues created my need for pain, not my own but the need to cause it. That was the psychobabble I heard when I was sixteen anyway. Maybe it's true. Doesn't matter. I am what I am, and figuring out why isn't going to change it. I like who I am.

I wipe the snot from my nose with the back of my free hand and open my eyes to stare at the handwriting.

S,

It was fun while it lasted, but we're not one of your products. We don't need your training. Don't try to find us. We don't want to be found by you.

Goodbye.

G

The curve of each letter, each dot—it's burned into my memory, but I can't stop looking at it. Do I hope that it'll reveal some hidden message? A hopeful note that I *should* find her and reclaim her?

Am I a fool because I still hope that she wants me? I still hope that what I feel for her—*all* of her, *each* of her—is reciprocated. I don't believe that it was just "fun" for her because I think that was only her anger and fear talking. I hope it was anyway.

She and I are alike, formed from what fate served us as a raw deal. I don't know what her history is or what made her how she is, but I know that she accepts herself, just as I do. I know that it's what drew me to her and her to me. I'm the answer to her pain. She's the answer to my need for it.

I don't give a shit what she says or how she feels. I realize that what I want may not be enough for her, but I know that she's everything that I need. I know I can make her see that I'm everything that's right for her.

She's mine. I'm hers.

Fuck my conscience.

San Francisco: Simon Lamb

The stillness of her apartment is what strikes me as strangest. It's like when I first went to her Chinatown apartment after she evaded me last year.

It's too calm, too quiet, too perfect. She obviously isn't here. It doesn't smell like her at all. Instead, there's only a scent of lemons and pine and something floral, not her.

But it's not the smell that tells me she isn't here. It's the perfect stillness—not her style.

I know this before my feet reach the end of her entrance rug, even before the door clicks soundly behind me, but I continue to walk in, keeping an ear out for any sounds anyway.

I know none of her friends have seen her. She hasn't been to any of the modeling gigs she had scheduled weeks ago.

She hasn't returned to her shitty apartment above the tea shop either. I didn't think she'd go there, but I checked anyway since it was on the way here.

I thought she'd be confident enough to come back, reaching out to her home and life here as she forgot about me or, perhaps, still seethed with anger. I thought she'd want to send me the message that she wasn't going to run away and hide; she was just done with me.

I thought *that* was her style.

Was I wrong?

The stillness is my only answer.

I can see that the place is kept clean and ready, so it's impossible to tell how long she's not been here. I can guess though. I have a sinking feeling that I let her slip through my fingers. Again.

Now that she knows I'm onto her secrets, she could be harder to find this time. She'll want to stay hidden from me as well as the past that had her hiding in the first place. Fuck.

Walking into her open kitchen, I don't hope to find anything but look in the fridge anyway. Only condiments and unopened bottles of water remain. I grab one and stand at her counter, drinking it.

The art above her sofa makes me grin though. I still have something similar above my bed. She's a terrible artist, but then again, she's a toddler doodling with crayons. This makes me smile more because I can picture her perfectly this way.

And it gives me some hope. She hasn't abandoned this place or even the Chinatown apartment. At least, I don't think she has.

I head into her bedroom to check if she packed up anything. The same stillness layers this room. It doesn't look like anything's missing from her closet, but there's so much shit in here that it's impossible to tell. I only see one suitcase on a shelf, but I have no idea if she has another one.

Fuck. I have no idea about a lot of shit. I sit on her bed and stare at her closet, trying to figure out my next move because waiting around for her to show is going to suck.

When I get up and turn around to leave, I see the note. Like a fucking moron, I didn't see it first? I don't dwell on yelling at myself, just quickly snatch it up. It takes reading it several times, or at least staring at it for a long time, to get the message through my head though.

Gillian and Miles—these names keep ricocheting in my mind.

And so much makes sense all at once that I sit back down on her bed, the note forgotten in my hand.

Red knew him. She talked to Miles, and she left with him. Fuck. She told me; Grace fucking told me that she belonged to him. I was just too clueless to know who she meant at the time—Miles.

But that doesn't make sense. I have a clear image in my head of both Red and Grace being afraid the night she left, but not of me. I was just too stupid to realize who made her afraid at the time—Miles.

Because if she knew Miles, that meant *he* was her past. And her past fucked her up. So he was at least part of what she was running from, hiding from. Right? Or did she run from me, back to him?

Fuck.

I pull my phone out and do what I should've done weeks ago. I check out what there is to know about Miles Vanderson online, and I could seriously hit myself for what I find. Instead, I settle for punching the wall with his fucking note crumpled in my fist.

The blood on my knuckles goes unnoticed because I'm moving too fast, my phone clutched in that hand. "Cary, I need your help with something."

Seattle: Simon Lamb

"Are you sure about this, cuz?" Cary nervously taps his thumbs on the steering wheel, not looking at me but staring at the line of trucks ahead of us instead.

I don't answer him; there's no need. I just check that the safety's off my Bersa .380 and put it back in the waistband of my pants, easily hidden under my jacket.

I haven't had target practice in months. Cary and I used to go with Grandfather on a hunting trip once a year, but keeping up with shooting hasn't been a priority for a long time now. I'm still pretty sure I could make any shot I aim at within 100 yards, maybe not with this gun, but I won't be 100 yards away either.

I realize that Cary is staring at me again, and he hasn't moved the truck through the open gates. "Drive, Cary." I nod towards the guard who is waving us forward. We finally get moving again, and I get my first look at the large Vanderson estate. Fuck, it's a beast.

Truthfully, I'm not sure about anything, but this is my only plan—get in, find her, and get my answers finally.

Seattle: Grace/Gillian

Gigi?

The stage is cold and empty. And it's too quiet.

It's too bright. I can see the edges. Or rather, I can't see any edges; it just goes on now.

Gigi!

I'm here, Grace. You don't have to shout.

I thought…I'm afraid.

I know you are. You'll be fine. Let's see how we look, okay?

I turn to face the large gold mirror leaning against the wall in our bedroom, and I think I look pretty. I know Gigi can see how we really appear, but I still prefer to see me as I am on the stage, as I've always seen myself, even if she makes fun of me for it.

The woman I see smile back at me is short with light caramel skin and freckles on high, round cheeks and a gently flattening nose. She has full pink lips, sparkling black eyes, and tight curls. I look nothing like our mother did, nothing like the pictures of Gillian Starck either…Gillian Vanderson, I correct myself.

And I'm glad that Miles agreed to let me wear red tonight. It's not my usual color of choice, but I see why Gigi likes it so much. It makes my dark coloring stand out. The dress also flatters my girlish figure in all the right places as I turn to see myself from different angles. The movement makes the bracelet sparkle. This draws my attention back to it and back to Gigi's plan.

Gigi, do you really think you'll be able to get this off?

I'm going to try since you can't find the key.

But if Miles finds out…

It's a risk we have to take, Grace.

Easy for you to say.

I know it isn't though. Gigi has a backup plan, and she doesn't like it any more than I do.

But with the house filling with people and noise for the party, it's now or never to try and run again. Miles hasn't left us alone for very long today, so I had to pretend taking my time in getting dressed. I had to feign excitement at being presented as his wife tonight.

Okay. I'm ready, Gigi.

Then I turn inside for the first time in weeks.

Seattle: Red/Gigi

Jesus. That's disorienting.

I take a deep breath and look away from our reflection. I don't think we've ever switched places in front of a mirror before. Grace only laughs at me.

Nice. I almost fell on my ass, Grace.

She only laughs harder through her hand over her mouth at that image, but it feels good to hear. It fills the empty stage with something at least.

She and I are the last two. All the Unknowns and others are no more. I know she's still upset with me for what I've done. She wants to deny that it was necessary. Lilly and Jill understood, though, before I took them. I think Grace does too, on some level, but she won't talk about it with me.

I know Lilly tried to explain it to Grace before she gave herself to me. She believed, as I do, that this is the only way. Lilly wasn't with me when I took Baby, but she knew how hard that was for me. Baby wasn't an Unknown. I loved her, just as I loved Lilly and Jill. And now they're all gone, but I know it was necessary. I'm stronger for it.

Grace said she'll only think about it if we can't get free, but then it'll be too late. The decision will be made for her; we'll be out of options. That's Grace for you though. She doesn't like to make up her own mind. She likes to splinter it instead.

That's the truth that lurked in the darkest corners of the stage. It's the truth I understood from that sandbox. She *is* the original Gillian, or she was. But she splintered and splintered and just kept splintering with each new sick episode with Mother, Miles and any other moment that was too much for her to bear alone.

I took all of that. I bear every one of those memories now, every one of hers.

And I faced my own biggest fear. I'm still me. I didn't break down or splinter or hide. I didn't become something else or *someone* else. I took it all, and I'm still me.

I'm more than me. I'm Them.

But I still fear what will happen if Grace is forced to face the truth. The truth we ran from three years ago is still the same one we face now. We can try to run, but Miles will never give up on her.

I also know something else that she doesn't want to face. I'm afraid too. I don't know which of us will be left standing if I have to take her back to that sandbox, if I have to force her to face all the memories she buried there. Grace is stronger than she thinks. I have no idea if I'm strong enough to overcome her will to survive at any cost.

Maybe it won't come to that. If I can get this damn shackle off my wrist, that is.

I head into the bathroom to look for something to use on the bracelet's clasp. At this point, I'm willing to break my fucking hand to get it off if I have to.

Seattle: Simon Lamb

"You sure you don't want me to go in with you?" This is about the tenth time Cary's asked me this.

I give him the same answer I have the last nine times— a shut the fuck up look. We're parked around back with all the other catering trucks. There are more people here than I expected, which is good and bad. It makes it easier to blend in and not be seen but harder to get away in a hurry if we need to. Something tells me that we're not going to be casually leaving by the front door.

"All right, but you know if you're caught," Cary doesn't finish the warning, just raises his eyebrows questioningly.

I didn't even have to ask him to drive. After I finally told him the full story, he only asked me what I planned to do. "I know if I'm caught, I'm going to need *your* ass out here to bail *my* ass out of jail." Trespassing, breaking and entering, illegal use and transport of a firearm, attempted kidnapping—yep, I can only hope for bail if this goes wrong.

My plan has a lot of flaws, but it's the best I could come up with on short notice. I doubt the opportunity to get into a fortress like this is going to present itself again anytime soon, at least not this easily.

Cary shrugs at the logic of my answer, but I stop him again from arguing. "And if you see any signs of police or trouble, you need to leave. Got it?"

"I'm not leaving you behind, cuz."

"Yes. You are."

He only grins, and I know he won't listen to me. I also know that he won't be stupid either. He'll follow my shitty plan and stay with the truck, only leaving if he sees me being hauled away in cuffs.

I open my door and step out. I have the same catering jacket as everyone else. That was the easiest part. One phone call three days ago and a very helpful servant told me that I was unfortunately too late to put in a bid for catering this party; Mr. Vanderson had already decided all the details. A little charm and I had all the information I needed to make

192 | WILLOW MADISON

up the fake sign on a truck and jackets to match the real staffers running around here.

"Hey!" I duck my head back into the truck, and Cary's still grinning at me. "Can I get your credit card?"

"What the fuck for?"

"Bail, of course."

"Fuck you." But I'm smiling as I slam the door closed.

The only good thing about my plan is that it isn't complicated. Hunt through the massive house until I find Grace—*Gillian*, I remind myself—and get her in the truck.

It's not like I haven't kidnapped a girl before, just not quite like this.

I've never been quite as blind about what I'll find or *who* she'll be.

34

Seattle: Miles Vanderson

Regret is not something I usually think about. I know it's a motivator for other people, but it never has been for me.

But I do now regret not waiting to give Gillian a big wedding here. This party will have to do, but I have a pang of disappointment in not having that moment of immense pride, seeing her walk to me in pristine white beauty as our guests can only look on. I missed out on that experience when she would give herself publicly to me, and everyone else would be witness to my possession of her.

I smile, adjusting my lapels and admiring the shine of my shoes as I head upstairs. I don't have regrets because I'm a man that knows how to get what I want one way or another.

I turn at the top of the first set of stairs and look back down at the wood paneled entrance. Staff and caterers are still running around, positioning flowers and trays and tables, polishing and sweeping and fussing. Spencer's security team mills around the front entrance, but not intrusively.

The space is large enough to accommodate all my guests. This will serve nicely. I can picture Gillian standing right here for the briefest moment before descending down to take my outstretched hand. All eyes will be on her as she makes her way to me slowly.

It's not the same as hearing her vows to be mine in front of everyone, but it will still be a show of her submissively giving herself to me. And all my guests will be witnesses when I kiss her tonight for the first time, and she blushes for me. I'm immensely hard thinking about that.

Another regret pops into my head to make my smile fade. I'll need to inform her that she has to change clothes. As I continue up to our room, my smile shifts to something more as the memory of our wedding night hits my crotch with a tightening effect. She can't wear *that* white dress again; it was left behind in tattered pieces. She has other white gowns that will be perfect, though, and I'll tear tonight's dress off her too.

Making my way up the stairs, I decide that every time she wears a white dress, I'll rip it off her as a reminder for us both of our fated love and the futility of trying to run from it.

Turning into our hallway, my pocket pings with three rapid beats, and I stop in my tracks. I'd almost forgotten the sound, but there's no mistaking that it's the alarm from her bracelet. I can see by the app that she hasn't moved; she must be trying to get it off.

I'm blind to my quick steps and the key in my hand already. I'm blind to the door slamming open and Gillian jumping in surprise. I'm blind to everything except her hands, one pushing down on the other.

And her eyes, she's not my Gillian.

Seattle: Red/Gigi

Shit. I have one second to make a choice, and I make the only one there is.

I rush at Miles. I push with all my body at full speed to knock him out of the way of the open door.

But he's not surprised. Miles is ready for me even.

The smile on his face crawls coldly up my back, shaking me more than his hands on my wrists that pull me off my feet.

He's so fucking calm and maniacal at the same time. I scream and kick and bite, anything to get away.

But he uses my own wrists and the bracelet to hit my head. The diamond cluster is a spike that pierces my right temple repeatedly with his words yelled into my cowering face, "You think you can get away?! You aren't ever getting away again! Ever!"

He finally stops when I sag against him, my legs giving up even as I try to push off him with my arms. He brings my wrists around to my back, and I see a flash of red over sparkle. We're both panting, held in this mockery of a loving embrace.

His voice is calm though, too calm. He's insanely calm. "*Gillian*. My love, we'll deal with this betrayal after the party. We have guests arriving soon, and you need to change."

He lets my wrists go slowly, and I wobble to stand on my own, the room spinning. I have an urge to fall to my knees, but I squeeze my nails into my palms to fight it off. I won't give him the satisfaction.

With one finger, he lifts my chin to meet his eyes, but I frown trying to focus on him this close. "I expect Gillian to be in a white dress with *this*," he moves his hand through my hair, bringing wet fingertips back down my cheek and neck, "this cleaned up. I'll be back in 20 minutes. That should be more than enough time for *you* to be gone."

He wipes the rest of my blood off his fingers onto my hip as he shoves me hard to the floor. I can only watch his legs recede and the door to my freedom close once more while I clutch the carpet and try to stay sitting up.

With the click of the key, I burst into a scream, an animal yell of frustration and anger and pain. My upper body shakes too much to be held by my weak elbows. I sink to the carpet and don't care that I'm openly sobbing now that I'm alone. More hot tears fucking wasted on him!

Seattle: Simon Lamb

I've traveled a lot. I know my way around a Sheik's desert palace, a Comte's hilltop villa, a tycoon's mountain lodge. My own home is large by any standard, but I've been wandering this fucking dark and depressing shithole for over thirty minutes with no sign of Miles or Gra—Gillian yet. And I've already been reprimanded twice for being where I shouldn't be since I'm dressed like a fucking servant.

Okay. Feel better, crybaby? Got it out of your system? I actually grin picturing how I'd be saying this to Cary if he were here with me. He wouldn't be able to contain his frustration either. I only hope he isn't getting into any shit parked outside for this long.

I'm slowly creeping my way through the east wing of the second floor when I finally spot Miles. Lucky for me, he isn't looking anywhere except his own hand and muttering something while marching quickly down the hall away from me.

I can see the door he just left and locked, and I have a pretty good idea who he's keeping in there too—my girl.

As I near the door, there can be no mistaking that she's inside. Her scream is loud enough to be heard downstairs, I think. I look to my right to see if Miles will return to shut her up but hear no sign of him. His staff is probably used to hearing things that they conveniently ignore. I should know; mine certainly does.

Right up next to the door, I loudly whisper, "Gra— Gillian?" Am I ever going to have only one name for her? No answer. "Red?" Still no answer. She probably can't hear me through the door, but I don't think she's right next to it.

It looks thick, and I know it's locked. This is gonna hurt. I move to the opposite side of the hall and brace my shoulder to take the door down, but I stop the running jump with one foot off the ground. I have an idea.

The door I'm against luckily isn't locked, so I open it and take a few steps inside. More dark and depressing in this room.

I turn around and brace myself again for the impact with the door, but I think the extra few feet should be enough now. I take the running jump and crash with a creak and loud "Fuck!" I fall into the room but stay on my feet, hopping and holding my shoulder. Surprisingly, the door is unharmed. Only the old deadbolt lock broke in two, the metal bolt falling to the carpet with a hard thump.

"Simon?" It's a cracked whisper, but my name never sounded better from her.

Still cradling my arm, I stop in front of her crumpled body in the center of the floor. "Did you think I'd let you get away from me that easily, sweetheart?" I grin at her confused look until I notice how dazed her eyes are and all the blood. There's fucking bloody streaks on her face, and drops speckle her shoulder and across the front of her dress. Oh God. Even more mats her hair to her face.

I slide to my knees and forget my arm, forget that the sound of me barging in here could be heard by anyone, forget anything else. I pull her more off the ground by her shoulders and force her to look into my eyes.

"Did he hurt you?"

Red laughs her gorgeous, can't get enough of it laugh, and I kiss her lips to capture it. Her tongue tries to meet mine, but she starts to slip back down, and it's then that I know she's hurt, even if she can't feel it.

"We need to get out of here. Can you walk, Red?"

She shakes her head, and I can see how her eyes narrow with the effort. I pull her closer to me and get my arms positioned to lift her, but she pushes me away. "No. You have to leave. Miles can't find you here."

"He won't find *us* here in a minute. Just hang on to me if you can." I pull her up more, but she resists again.

"No. He'll have you arrested if he finds you." Her voice isn't as strong, pressed against my shoulder. I can feel her wet lips and tears through my shirt and jacket, and it brings to mind the image of her in my bed the last time her lips wrapped around me. Get a grip, not the time!

"I know. That's why we need to leave. Now."

This time she manages to push harder from me, freeing herself enough to stare into my eyes. "Not for being here. For the other shit, the girls you took and trained. He knows about that, and he'll use it against you if he finds out you came here."

It's my turn to laugh, but it's more of a grunt. "Is that why you left with him? The night you left me with nothing but that fucking note?" She only nods slightly, the anger and pain on my face pretty obvious, I'm sure. "I don't need you to protect me, sweetheart. I just need you to grab on to my shoulders because I am getting you the fuck out of here now."

She laughs in response, and it's a laugh I hope never to hear again, sad and low. Her voice is lower too and flat. "And what good will you be to me if you're behind bars, knowing Miles will use whatever means to get me right back here?"

She's staring at me, but her eyes are a little different— more calculating yet innocent somehow. "Red?" It's so not the time for her to be tripping through personalities.

Her smile is pure Red though—seductive, dipping up and down so her cheeks rise more than her lips part. "My name is Gigi, but you can always call me Red, Trust."

Great, another name, but I smile at her. I like the sound of her name and how her eyes sparkle when I say it. "Well, Gigi, time for you to be a good girl and stop arguing with me. We're leaving. Now."

She only shakes her head, a little less wobbly at the motion at least. "I have a plan, and if it works, maybe then we can be together."

I look her over. The blood on her head and face has darkened, her thick dark curls crusting with it. Her eyes are clearer though, and I know she isn't feeling any pain. I look at her hands on my chest and see what he used to beat her. Both her wrists are turning shades of black, especially her left one under the large bracelet.

I take her hands in mine and bring her fingers up to my lips to gently kiss. "You really think I'm leaving here without you?"

She only smiles sweetly, almost Grace's sweet smile but somehow even softer like her voice. "I think you have no choice."

I'm almost whispering when I reply, "That's my line." And at that, I pick her up easily, squeezing her hands against my chest so she can't push away.

"How nice. Gillian, you didn't tell me we have a visitor."

Fuck. I slowly turn around and see Miles standing in the doorway; his dark eyes are lit with a crazy intensity, and his mouth twitches. The man I saw weeks ago is gone. This isn't a man trying to stay in control or be an intimidating son of a bitch. He's a crazy fuck who won't take losing easily— a man who's no longer even pretending to have his shit together; he doesn't need to any longer.

But I'm holding his prize, and I'm not letting go.

Seattle: Red/Gigi

He came for us?! Gigi? Simon came for us! Please... Please, just go with him.

We can't, Grace. Don't you know that? He'd be fucked.

I only know that I'm scared. And I'm alone in here. Please! Please, don't leave me alone in here! Please don't leave me alone with Miles again!

Shhh, I'm here. Shhh. You're not alone, I promise. I won't ever let Miles hurt you again, Grace. I promise. You're safe. Just stay calm, okay?

I get only silence in return.

A feeling of despair and fear threatens to overwhelm me. A black yawning expanse of pure emptiness pushes back against the light in the corners of the stage. I know that feeling well. I know there will be new Unknowns to give themselves up to me again. Unless I act fast. Unless I put a stop to Grace splintering more.

She's right though; Simon did come for us. I knew those pictures of him were lies. I could see the look on his face, through the haze of liquor and drugs. I saw how his fingers curled while around those girls. I saw how he stopped himself from really touching them. I knew he still felt me, us, in his heart. I knew he still wanted me. There was sadness in his eyes.

And he's here now, kissing me, lifting me, wanting me.

Oh, God. Simon! I can't let you be a part of this!

I push against him but too late. Our fate is sealed once more.

Seattle: Miles Vanderson

I knew what I'd find before I even entered the room. I heard it all; their twisted reunion, so sad and sweet, broadcast loud and clear over the bracelet's application.

Seeing how Lamb clutches at her, how her eyes look up to him like he's her savior, provokes a rage I haven't felt since the night I came home to find her missing three years ago. It actually surpasses even that fury because this is thrice the betrayal now. She means to run from me again and with him this time.

I take two deep breaths to still the impulse to hit him where he stands. It won't do to lose my temper now. I'll have my security detain him and rough him up before the police arrive. I smile with this plan.

"*Gillian*. Our guests will be arriving soon. You need to change, *my* love." I'm impressed at how levelheaded I can sound when inside I'm boiling with rage.

Gillian only laughs one gasp of air out, but she twists to get away and obey me. Lamb finally lowers her feet back to the floor.

"She's not going anywhere with you, Miles." Lamb sounds like he's failing to get control of his own anger, pulling my Gillian back and holding her against his side. I know she's not Gillian, not yet. Her eyes blaze at me, but that doesn't matter. I know my Gillian is inside there, and I know she'll obey me as she always has.

"She's my wife, and she'll go where I tell her to. Won't you, Gilli?"

There's a burgeoning look of surprise on Lamb's face at this. He glances down at her hands and quickly up at her eyes. She only shrugs slightly in his hold against the obvious question in his expression.

His jaw is set when he looks back to me. "I don't care if you did trick her into marrying you. She's leaving here with me. Get out of our way."

I smile, still amazingly composed in the face of this infuriating conversation. "I fail to see how she'll leave with you when *you*, Mr. Lamb, will be leaving with the police." I pull my phone from my pocket with a wider smile.

I falter, though, when I see that Lamb has pulled a gun. I look from him to Gillian and see her shock as well. She pushes away from him, but he doesn't ease his hold on her.

"Drop the phone, Miles, and kick it over here." Lamb sounds a lot calmer now. I suppose holding the upper hand will do that for a man.

I laugh, though, because he's still clueless about the real power exchange here. I drop my phone with a bouncing thud on the thick carpet and easily kick it towards Gillian, not taking my eyes off her. "*Gilli*, my love, I'll give you two seconds to tell this man that he's wrong about you, that you don't want to leave with him at all."

Simon laughs this time, but the gun doesn't even dip in his loose grip. His aim never wavers, not even when Gillian pushes harder against him to free herself.

Seattle: Simon Lamb

Red laughs once with a snort as she pushes herself to standing, my arm only loosely around her. I don't take my eyes off Miles, but I can feel her shaking with more crazed laughter that threatens to become unbottled quickly.

I put as much authority as I can into my voice, one I hope she'll respond to. It's one I know Grace and the others would anyway. "Take it easy, Red. We'll be out of here soon, sweetheart."

The satisfying initial look of shock and fear on Miles'
face is gone, but her laughter has him frowning.

"Gilli, as you call her, won't be doing anything that
you tell her to ever again, Miles." Damn, but her strong,
husky voice shoots my dick straight up. I have to smile when
I see that it has the opposite effect on Miles.

He looks from me to her quickly. He seems to
completely ignore the fact that I'm aiming a gun only a few
feet from him and manages to sound in control, addressing
only her. "I'll give you to the count of two to get yourself
under control, *Gillian*. One."

I laugh at this, but Red answers him—no laughter in
her voice, almost a sadness. "It's no use, Miles. You'll never
have what you want. *I* won't let you. But because I know
that her love for you will always be something that I'll have
to live with, I'll let you have a goodbye. It's more than you
deserve, but it's not for you."

And I feel her change. I keep my eyes on Miles, but I
don't need to look at her to know that Grace is leaning
against me now.

Seattle: Miles Vanderson

I watch as my sweet Gillian moves out from under his arm. Blinking, she stands only feet from me, her soft stillness adding an odd ethereal quality to this surreal scene: two men, one gun, and one girl. One messed up girl.

I know now that Lamb does know about her personality issues. He didn't blink an eye at her little speech or at the obvious change in her, but that doesn't matter. He may know this much about her, but he doesn't really know *her*, not like I do. He's still clueless.

I smile and put my hand out for Gillian to take, and she reaches for me. Lamb grabs her arm and commands her, "Stay where you are, Grace. I may have to shoot him, baby, and I wouldn't want you to get in the way." His lips sneer with his threat, but I can see that he's serious. He intends to shoot me if he thinks he needs to.

The thought sends a thin wave of fear through my body but surprisingly doesn't register as more than a small threat. No, the real threat is his hand on Gillian's arm and her obedience to his command.

My voice darkens and lowers. "Gillian, tell Mr. Lamb to get his hand off you. Tell him who you *really* belong to."

Tears slip beautifully down her cheeks and make her dark eyes shine even more. "I'm sorry, Miles. Please don't be angry with me." Her voice is soft and almost child-like, shaking. Not her usual pleading voice, but I like it. She moves one foot toward me, and Lamb squeezes her arm harder, stopping her other foot from following.

She turns her eyes up to him, and he looks down for one blink before refocusing on me. "I'm sorry, Simon. You shouldn't be here. You should leave. I can't go with you. I told you before, I belong to Miles."

I smile warmly at the blood draining from Lamb's face, but he recovers quickly. "No. You don't, Grace. Fuck." He doesn't lower the gun, but he turns his head more to look at her. "I don't know what this sick fuck did to you, but I can guess it has a lot to do with how you are. And I'm *not* leaving you with him."

"She already told you to leave. Now, *I'm* telling you to leave, Mr. Lamb." I take a step toward her. "Gilli, pick up my phone and press 2 for our security."

I think Lamb's in such shock that he actually lets her slip out of his hand and bend down for the phone. But she hesitates, staring at it, her look clouded and frowning as if in pain. "Don't do it, Grace. I'll get us out of here, but you need to trust me."

"I'm the only man that she trusts, Lamb." I laugh as he appears uncertain of his next move, frowning at her but not moving to grab her again. "Isn't that right, my love?" Her eyes lift up to me, but she's still unfocused, dazed like when I stopped hitting her with her own wrists earlier. "I'm the only one who understands you, who knows what you need to feel safe and loved." I take another step towards her, but she stays motionless, a deer in my headlights.

I know I have her again.

The Stage: Red/Gigi

Her body responds as it always has, and Grace gives in to it as she always did.

I gained a greater perspective of her from the safari. I always knew my place among the others, but it wasn't until I'd stolen *all* their memories as my own that I fully understood the strengths we each possessed.

I know Baby hid behind her helpless need for innocence. It made dealing with life's horrors easier for her if she could crawl away from it and only have the memories of quiet mornings to play by herself. She didn't have to see Mother or all the other men and women that made our lives hell during the first seven years. The pain of our lives never touched her that way, and Baby's laughter never died.

I know Jill hid behind her ugly need for destruction. She would throw her tantrums when no one was watching and feel a sense of calm after seeing how she could destroy something, have some measure of control over what was around her. It made the next seven years easier to bear when Mother became more focused and singular in her sickness. Pain became anger, and Jill's will to not give in never died.

I know Lilly hid behind her thirsty need for knowledge. It became a distraction against the violence and made all the years leading up to this one easier to fade into memories that were trumped by learning something new. Pain became secondary, and Lilly's reach to be more never died.

And I know I hid behind my hungry need for pleasure. Taking what was painful and making it mine, it was the only control I had, and I grasped it from the beginning. Finding gratification from being able to transcend the physical, while not giving in to what I couldn't control, it's the only thing that saved us through the worst of times. Pain became desire, and my passion never died.

But Grace has always hid behind her simple need for love. A love she once received in answer to her tears in a sandbox long gone from her memories. She's never even tried to not submit to it. Pain became the reason to hide, the reason to splinter, and Grace's fears never died.

I hated her for that. I laughed at her. I pitied her for it even.

Now, from the stage, I can only watch as she does what she must. I can feel my nonexistent tears as they slide down my nonexistent cheeks, matching the real ones shed by Grace. I don't know if I cry for her or me. Or Them.

I was good at staying in control; I only ever lost a little when I tried to get something more than just pleasure. When I let myself foolishly believe that Miles wanted more than absolute control, I thought I could love him and he'd love me. Love doesn't work like that though. I know that now.

But Grace never learned that lesson, and she never will. Her heart can't be broken because she refuses to let it. She takes whatever is offered as love, even the sick and twisted version that Miles insists in devoting to her.

And she can't help but submit to him now. Even as fear is trembling through her body, her feet move to take his still outstretched hand.

I feel a few grains of sand on a wind that is starting up again.

Seattle: Grace/Gillian

"Grace. Don't."

I stop, uncertain of what to do. Simon moves his hand as if to take my arm again, and I can see Miles narrow his eyes, his fingers twitching in agitation for me to take them.

"I love you, Gilli. Haven't I always taken care of you?" Miles' voice is soft, but his eyes are hard and only getting darker. I shrink with the fear I know he wants me to feel.

"Yes." Even to my own ears, my voice is faraway and soft. Gigi is silent; the stage is silent.

Miles' lips are soft and relaxed as he smiles at me. I move another foot toward him. "And haven't I always protected you?" I only nod, fixed on his lips that still smile, slightly parted. I know I'm pleasing him, doing what he wants. I bring my left hand up but hesitate at seeing blood and the darkness spreading at my wrist.

"Gillian." I lift my eyes back to his lips quickly. "Didn't I make sure that your mother never hurt you again?" I nod once more. "And you gave yourself to me. You promised to always be mine and mine alone. Didn't you?"

I nod once more and move toward Miles again.

I gasp with the grasp on my arm from behind and the shock of my body slamming against Simon's in a move that has me off my feet for a moment. I'm pinned against Simon's side, with his arm around my stomach and my toes barely touching the floor. I can't breathe and gasp more until he slowly lets me go enough to stand on my feet again.

"That's enough, Miles," Simon's voice booms over my head.

"Let her go, Lamb. She's not yours, and she knows it even if you don't." Miles laughs. "Look at her. Look at how she tries to get free and come to me even now." And I am pushing against Simon's arm with all my might, not getting him to budge at all. "You can walk out of here, and I'll forget all about this mess. I'll let you go and live your life and trap whatever girl you want next. I don't care, but Gillian stays. She belongs to *me*."

Seattle: Simon Lamb

I don't know what the fuck is going on here—why Grace is willingly walking to this asshole—but I don't care either.

I'll deal with her fucked up mind when we're away from here and away from the fuck that obviously did more than hurt her physically.

I look down and see Grace still struggling in my arm, but it's her tears on my hand that I feel.

I've trained a lot of women. I've broken them down and rebuilt them, but I've taken a certain pride in leaving just enough of their own selves in place to be what any man would want—what my clients don't even know they really want when they come to me looking for a product.

I give my clients exactly what they demand as far as specific fetishes and likes or dislikes, but I leave enough of a woman's heart and soul intact to be a willing and intelligent participant in all things pleasurable, painful and not. I've never broken a woman down so deeply that she's nothing but a shell, nothing but a bundle of nerves that recede from pain and leap to anything close to comfort.

I see now that this is what Grace is. This is why she's been the perfect submissive for me. She's responded to me in every way exactly as she thought I wanted, with little thought to what would be her own desires or needs.

I feel my stomach churn with the realization that I've hurt her in the same way Miles has, even if I didn't know it before. I thought Grace gave herself to me out of a deeper understanding of what we share—that she knew what I needed from her was the softness she offered, that I needed how she didn't judge me for any of the darkness inside me.

"She doesn't belong *to* you, asshole. She belongs *with* me. Step one more fucking toe near her, and I'll blow your Goddamn kneecap off before I put a bullet between your eyes to end your miserable ass life."

I have the satisfaction of seeing Miles' face blanch and his hand fall to his side. Grace also calms against me.

But in an instant, I know it's not Grace anymore. It's Red again, and thank fucking God because she's at least on board with getting away from here. I think.

And I can suppress the guilt I feel over Grace a little longer because I don't have this guilt with Red. She *is* my match; of that, I'm certain.

Miles laughs. "You fire that gun and I'm at least going to die with the knowledge that you'll spend the rest of *your* 'miserable ass life,' as you so crudely put it, Mr. Lamb, behind bars because my security will be up here before you can reach the landing." His sarcasm and smug smile have me itching to pull the trigger, but his words make me take stock of the situation again.

I need to get Red out of here without calling attention to us. Fuck. How exactly am I going to do that with a houseful of guards and servants and this fuck in the way?

Some plan, jackass.

Grandfather's words of caution against my impulsiveness have me itching to shoot something again.

The Stage: Red/Gigi

Grace. It's time.

I don't want to. Please don't make me...

I don't like it either, but we can't let Miles win. We can't let him hurt Simon.

I won't do it...

Sorry. It has to be done, Grace. You know that, don't you?

Sand swirls all around now. I reach out my nonexistent hands and pull Grace to me. She doesn't struggle much, submitting to me the same as she always did.

The cyclone starts, and we're ripped to pieces.

Seattle: Red/Gigi

"He's right, Simon." I feel his hand loosen against my ribcage, and for a moment, I imagine us in bed like we were only weeks ago. His arms and legs were tangled with mine, his lips on my shoulder and his cock pressed into my ass. I close my eyes for a second and smile at how fucked up my mind can be to have this image now, to have my body respond with pressing against him in the middle of all of this.

But I take the strength I've gained from Grace. It's the strength to let go of what I can't control and to only give in to it.

"Red? Gigi?" I nod and step out of Simon's arm. But when I turn to look into his beautiful blue eyes, I'm startled to see a little pain etched in his face. I know it's for Grace and trace just one finger along his jaw before leaning up to gently kiss his lips, barely pressing us together.

He seems startled by it and looks down at me, but I realize the error in taking our eyes off Miles. I know he's nowhere close to giving up. Yet.

I whirl around and smile at Miles, but all sweetness is gone. I'll mourn what Grace had for him, what I had for him. Maybe later...maybe someday. Of that I'm sure, but not now. Not today. Not while he could still hurt Simon.

"Give *me* the gun, Trust." Simon tenses behind me; Miles tenses in front of me. "You need to leave. I'll find you again when I can. Or you'll find me. But you need to leave now."

Neither man makes a move. I impatiently put my hand out, keeping my eyes leveled on Miles. I can see his wheels turning.

"*Gillian.*" His voice is a low growl, one I know normally precedes his usual fury when he's not just exercising his sadistic pleasures but he's actually angry about something one of us did. It's the tone that always meant that he would shed more than just our tears; he was out for blood. "I was going to have you spend a week in your cell for this latest betrayal, but if you keep this up, you'll spend a month in there." His lips shoot up into a half-smirk, and I'm almost transfixed watching them. "But if you behave now and come to me, all will be forgiven, my love."

I laugh, and it's a low throaty laugh that feels good because it's all mine. "I don't think so, Miles." I put my hands on my hips, a stance that I know pushes my tits out and gives me a feeling of being centered and ready for anything. I learned to stand like this from Jill, watching her brace herself for an angry fit. I smile because she would have liked what I'm about to say. They all would have…maybe even Grace.

I shake my head against the sadness thinking of her elicits and focus on his lips, just like Grace would have. I can muster more anger seeing the smugness pinched within his perfect petals. "There is no more Gillian, and for the record, her name was *Grace*, asshole." I laugh again and tap my fingers against my hips, liking how his eyes can't help but go to them.

I also like the little bit of fear I can see in him. Miles is only just figuring out what I'm saying, but I know when it really sinks in, he'll be done. My victory will be bittersweet but still a win for me, for Them, for us.

"Simon, you're going to leave now, and you're going to give me the gun. I'm going to shoot this sorry son of a fucking whore's breath, and then I'm going to delight when the police come to question me. Because you, my sweet stepbrother, my oh so how I tried to give my heart to Miles…you had doctors come here. You had doctors try to *fix* me, but they'll tell the police how they failed. They'll say how unstable I am. They'll testify that I'm nutty and not capable of right or wrong. And I may rot in a padded room for a little while…but I've had worse accommodations, haven't I?" I smile at his shocked look. "And Simon…he'll get me out…or I'll get myself out…but one way or another, you'll be fucking rotten meat in the ground, Miles."

I smile more at the increased fear I can see pinching his face, all his features twitching with comprehension. For the first time, he gets that he's not in control of me, and we both get that I could actually go through with shooting him.

I know that I would deal with the pain of the memory later, not as a separate someone but as me. I could do that now.

Seattle: Red/Gigi

"Afraid I'm not handing over the gun, Red. So if you want this asshole shot, just give me the word, sweetheart. We'll figure out the police and doctors and shit later."

My smile softens for a moment as I feel the pull that Grace would have to back down, to give in to both of the men in this room, but this isn't the time for softness. "What's it going to be, Miles?"

The twitching that started in Miles' face has moved down his body, but he manages to keep his voice steady and regains control of himself quickly. He ignores Simon, and the full focus of his stare startles me and makes me want to step back. "I'm not letting you just walk out of here, Gillian, or Grace, or whatever you want to call yourself. I know you think that running away is the answer, but it's always been our fate to be together, from that first moment in the library. You remember? Of course you do." And I smile sadly along with him at the memory of our first touch. "I'm not letting you go. I love you."

Before I can answer, Simon moves quickly, taking the step that brings him in between Miles and me. I hear the thud of knees hitting the floor before I see Miles slowly sink down, blood on the side of his head. His eyes are shocked and blanking as he lands on the carpet.

I watch Simon quickly put the gun in his back waistband, tucking his jacket over it. I'm shocked by how calm I am watching all this. My heart is racing and seems so loud to my ears that I have a hard time hearing Simon until he's shaking me by my shoulders.

"Red! Gigi! Come on, sweetheart, stay with me. Don't you dare faint on me." He smiles when I finally lift my eyes to his, hearing what he's saying for the first time again.

"Is he…?"

Simon shakes his head. "I only hit him with the gun."

I feel relief at knowing that Miles is still alive and fear at knowing that my one chance at real freedom is gone.

Simon seems to understand my quick thoughts, but his smile only hardens. "Change of plans." His cool lips press a kiss to my forehead.

Seattle: Red/Gigi

I hold my elbows, squeezing my arms around myself a little harder. I'm sitting on the bench next to the bed that has been my prison on and off for six years, in the home that has been my prison for that same length of time. The blanket that was always so neatly spread over the foot of the bed is draped over my shoulders. I don't remember who put it there.

I don't wince while a man to my right applies a strong smelling antiseptic to my temple before putting tape and a bandage there to cover what Miles did to me.

I watch in silence as the man I now know as Spencer marches into the room. He's with another man I don't know but think of as Detective 100. The house is crawling with them.

I keep my expression impassive through their questions, as I have for the last several hours. I keep my voice steady as I answer everything again, as I have for the last several hours too.

I stay composed as I listen to these men tell me that they found Miles' phone. They found his laptop. They found the application that tracks my every move. They found the live feed footage that documented the last weeks of punishments and confinement. They found the locked room.

They didn't find the key for the bracelet, but they're sending someone up to get it off for me.

They didn't find Miles, but they're still looking. They tell me that he's obviously unstable, and they're leaving police and security to keep an eye out for him.

And I stay blank, safely tucked away in my mind.

The stage is gone. It's no longer a place with light and dark shadows. It's a crystal clear pool of water that I wade into and feel the warmth as small waves caress my body.

There's no end to the water, no night or day, only the sound of soothing waves. It's a safe and peaceful place.

I smile at the man that comes to unlock me. He frowns at the bruises and swelling under the bracelet, but I tell him it doesn't hurt. He's gentle anyway.

Epilogue

"Hi, honey, how was work today?" My lips curl into a delicious smile, and my left leg, bent at the knee, sways back and forth, beckoning Simon to come closer. My long, dark curls provide a good cover over my bared breasts. The tendrils draw his eyes down the length of my exposed body, over my flat stomach rising and falling with my excited breathing, then back up to my nipples poking out between their silky hiding place. My leg continues to gently rock, giving him just a glimpse of the smooth lips between my thighs.

"Legs spread, Red. You know the rule." Simon's voice is strong and commanding as usual, but it also betrays his weariness. I slowly lower my feet on the cool sheets, keeping my legs pressed together to enjoy the pulsing between them for a second longer. In a quick swish across the silken sheets, I open my legs, toes pointed and back arched off the bed a little, just as he likes.

He stands at the end of the bed, admiring me, a smile playing across his lips as he takes me all in. His stare is as hungry for me as I am for him, but I can see the lines between his brows from time spent frowning with effort.

I don't know how long I've been tied to his headboard. I have had no sense of time, only of longing and need. The silky rope that binds me in place has enough give to allow me some movement, and my feet have been free to be naughty in coming together. But I've had no chance at getting away or doing anything except await Simon's pleasure.

The sheets are tossed off, and the blanket is kicked to the end. I've been wickedly trying to achieve an orgasm with the pressure and movement of my thighs and ass for a while now. I can smell Simon on the pillows that prop me up; I can smell myself in the air from the heat of my movements. It's our usual combination of spicy and sweet, and I mimic him as he takes a deep breath in through his nose, reminded of an animal hunting down prey.

I watch as he removes his black t-shirt. I know he showered before he came to me; he always does. Water droplets fall from his blond hair onto his muscled chest, and I strain with the desire to lick their path. His white teeth show as he licks his lips; Simon knows my thoughts.

My eyes follow the lines of his arms and stomach as he flexes with movement to remove his black lounge pants and shoes. He's without underwear, and I'm treated to a full view of his cock. He's hard, as he always is.

"Making good progress. I left Cary to finish up today." I can hear the darkness in his voice, the depth that only hints at what he won't share but I know still. And when his eyes drag up my body, I close mine against the wave of that darkness. It's a match to mine, a wave that we'll ride together.

"Look at me, Gigi." His commands. His voice. Him. I melt against the bed with the desire to comply, to obey, to give. I know what he needs, what *we* need, and it's not my softness right now that he craves. I keep my eyes closed.

The sound of the leather crop slicing the air strikes me first; the heat spreads across both my nipples at once. I open my eyes and mouth to let out one low moan. I'm met with his smile, and the darkness recedes for a moment.

He pushes my hair off my breasts with the crop, but he hesitates, tracing the red line without striking again. I only wait quietly.

His voice is so low, but it startles me; watching his hand move back and forth was almost hypnotic. "I think it'll be another week. I have a buyer in Durban lined up, a friend of a friend."

I only nod, still watching and waiting. He clears his throat, coming out of whatever thoughts he isn't sharing. "I'll need to deliver the product myself as usual, but I have that arranged. Cary will stay here with you." I nod once.

He's silent for so long that my mind wanders back to a day six months ago.

"Miles is insane, Red. I could hear it in his words, see it in his eyes." I nod my agreement, looking down at the body of the man who first had my heart.

"He'd never let you go. He'd see you destroyed, locked away, before he'd let that happen." Simon was right. Miles had wanted me, a different me, all to himself. He had wanted me to be ruled by all my pain, wanted to control me with it. I can only nod again, not taking my eyes off Miles. He hasn't moved, but Simon has.

He closes the bedroom door quickly and comes back to stand between Miles and me, taking my arms in a light squeeze of his hands. I pull my eyes up to his and am surprised to see Simon smiling. It's a real smile, eyes twinkling, lips open. I can only blink in return. "I can't let that happen, sweetheart. I won't let you pull the trigger and destroy yourself to gain your freedom from this piece of shit."

I smile at that. "Let me, Trust?"

He grabs my chin but gently, his eyes moving back up to the gash on my head. "Yes. Let you." His eyes change, and his whole body tenses, a shift that I counter with softening into him more. "I need to know some things first."

"Shoot." I raise an eyebrow and get a small smile out of him for my sarcasm. Remarkably, I'm still very poised with everything that's happened. I think it's Lilly's influence, and that makes me both sad and happy, lost for a moment in my own thoughts.

Simon relaxes a little, but his hand stays on my chin, keeping my eyes locked on his, keeping my focus on him. "Is Grace really gone?"

I can only nod against his hand for a moment, swallowing with the effort to say it out loud. "They're all gone." He nods too, running his hand over my cheek and catching tears I didn't know were falling.

He stiffens more. "Do you still think you belong to Miles? Do you still love him?"

I smile that this is what he wants to know, in the middle of this seriously fucked up situation, but Simon's frown darkens at me taking too long to answer. I lean into him and reach for his lips to kiss me softly, but he doesn't respond. Instead, he growls into my mouth, "Answer me."

"There's a part of me…of her…that…" I shake my head trying to make sense of what I feel. I decide to say only what I'm sure of right now. I'll sort the rest out later. "That's my past. I don't belong to my past anymore, Simon."

He smiles and relaxes again before yanking me into his arms and planting a big kiss on my lips, pulling away, then smashing back into me like he can't get enough of my tongue. With his forehead pressed to mine, his words are lustful and take my breath away. "Am I your future then, Gigi? Do you belong to me?"

My own lust boils my words to almost a painful depth, hot air more than syllables. "Is that what you want?"

His nod moves our heads together in a slow up and down. "Say it. Say you belong with me, to me."

"Yes. We belong together, Trust. We belong to each other." His lips trace their way down my face, over my eyelid, nose, cheek, lips, ending on my neck and making me squeal with a small bite.

He pulls away and grabs his phone from his back pocket, a strained smile starting on his set face. He turns back to Miles' body. "I'm going to get this shitbag out of here, and you're going to do exactly as I tell you to, Red."

I grab his shoulder and force him to turn back to me. "Don't push me, Trust. You can't just order me around. What the fuck are you going to do with him?"

His smile spreads, and he kisses my nose, ignoring my question as his call is answered. "Second floor, east wing. There's a close elevator by the door near you. Bring the cart. And, Cary, don't get noticed by anyone."

He ends his call and puts his phone back. Then he puts his arms around me, low at my waist, pushing our hips together. "Do you trust me?" I nod. His eyes move over my face. "You look like shit."

I slug his shoulder, but he smiles. "No. It's good. We'll use it." He kisses the frown between my brows, then lets me go to open the door a little and keep a lookout. I only stand, staring from him to Miles, unsure of what to do.

I watch as Cary moves inside quietly with a cloth covered tray table. He takes in Miles on the floor and the blood on me without saying a word. I notice, for the first time, that he and Simon are dressed in matching jackets.

"You were planning to kidnap me?"

Simon smiles as he closes the door quietly. "Get him on the cart. We need to move fast." When Cary lifts the side of the cloth, I can see rope and duct tape hidden on a lower shelf.

"Everything one needs for an abduction..." I stand with my hands on my hips, my sarcasm unanswered by either man.

Simon grins, though, as he ties the rope around Miles, tucking his arms and legs into a tight ball to keep his body hidden under the small table. Cary helps lift Miles, and the metal trays clang with his deadweight.

Simon stands up, and Cary finishes with the tape and pushing Miles into a better position.

Putting his hands on my shoulders, running them down my arms to pull my hands off my hips and onto his, Simon leans down to look into my eyes. "I told you before I won't give you choices. I wasn't leaving here without you, Red." But I see the softness in his smile too. I see his need for softness in return...a softness that I'm still not used to having or giving.

"Thank you for coming for me."

He kisses me, but Cary breaks us up. "Hey, can we get a move on here, cuz. You two can fuck in the van if you want."

"She's staying." I start to open my mouth. Cary does too, but Simon cuts us both off. "Are there surveillance cameras here?"

I shake my head. "No. Only in the cell."

I watch Simon's jaw tic for a moment. "He kept you locked up?" I can only nod against the fury I see in his eyes. He shakes it away, focusing on me again. "You're going to wait twenty minutes, then stumble out of here. Find anyone and tell them that Miles struck you. It'll be obvious, but make sure that you sound disoriented, confused. Say he hit you and then ran out of here. He sounded crazed and maniacal and ranted about jealousy and crap. Make up whatever. Say you passed out, and you don't know how long he's been gone or what he's capable of. Can you say all that?"

I nod. "The police will come. He has security everywhere. They'll investigate."

"Good. They'll find a battered wife, a sick fuck with a torture chamber, and nothing else." He kisses my forehead. "This is important, Red. Do not contact me in any way. I'll let you know when it's safe. You just keep up the appearance of an upset wife with a missing, crazy husband. Can you do that?"

I nod again and almost cry when he kisses me once briefly before following Cary out the door, closing it quietly behind him. I jump when he comes back in quickly, searching the floor. He stoops and picks up the metal chunk from the door's lock, putting it in his pocket. He rushes to me and grabs me for a hug and another quick but deeper kiss. "I'm never letting you go, Gigi. We'll be together soon, sweetheart. Just hold on."

His words were echoes of what Miles said so many times before. They contained all the same love, all the same possessiveness, all the same desire that Miles had for Grace.

And I know they contained all the same craziness too. Only a man crazy in love could do what Simon's done for me.

I followed his plan. I played the foolish wife with the insane husband. I let every detail of my life with Miles and Mother come out. I showed the police the room that was hidden, the cameras that were aimed. I showed them the bracelet that tracked. I let them examine me and see the fresh and old wounds. I was serene through their horrified stares, telling and retelling the same story.

The news reports were brutal. I refused all photos, interviews and comments. But they crucified Miles and made me a martyr, a saint, a victim anyway.

With no leads, no new information, the police stopped asking questions eventually. It's still an ongoing investigation, but I was granted a no-fault divorce with very little fuss.

I changed my name. It was all I could do to honor Martin Vanderson's memory and mourn the tarnish I had inflicted on his great name and empire. I officially became Gigi Grace Martin a few months ago.

And still, I waited to hear from Simon. I stayed in Seattle and bought a small condo to make it look like I was starting over, moving on. I kept to myself and didn't go out, so not much of my life changed for a while. I was still locked away because of Miles. I was still in hiding because of him.

Simon finally came for me a few weeks ago. He said his plan was close to being finished, and he needed me.

I'd never heard anything more beautiful. And I cried in his arms while he undressed me and entered me quickly. Like when this craziness all started, we were standing up, pressed to a wall, too hot for each other to remove all our clothes or let any space come between us for even a second.

His need for me was evident in his quick thrusts and deep moans, muffled against a bite on my shoulder. It was the first time that I didn't come during sex, but I got what I needed out of it. I had my Trust against me, kissing me and telling me we'd never be apart again.

He drove me to his home that day, straight through. He carried me up to his bed, and without any words, we started our future. I undressed and laid myself out for him, much as I am now. And he opened his cabinet and selected his favorite whip. I more than made up for not having an orgasm during our initial reunion that night and into the next day.

I smile at him now with the memory of how many times he made me scream his name. The next night, entwined in us and blankets and sweat, Simon said he needed to hear my cries, needed to have them filling his head.

I knew what he meant. I saw the pills in the bathroom. I know the price he's paying for me. He won't let me see, but I know.

His eyes are still watching me, moving over me as lazily as his crop, but he responds to my smile with one of his own. "You are the most beautiful woman I've ever seen, Gigi." He sits down next to me, and for a second, I can truly see how tired he is before he grins again. "I thought I'd wait to say this, until I was back, but I need to say it now."

I bring my foot up to playfully push at his shoulder. "Don't you think I already know, Simon?"

His eyes are rimmed with red, and he blinks several times. Breathing heavily, his voice is almost angry. "Okay. Then I need to say it for *me*. I need *you* to hear it. *I* fucking need to hear it."

I smile, and it's the softness of Grace, the memory of her, that fills my own eyes with tears because I'm filled now with all her needs too, all that drove her. It's my need now, and it constricts my voice, a lump in my throat. "Okay. Go."

Leaving the crop on my stomach and between my breasts, Simon takes my face in both his hands. He's gentle and sweet, staring between my eyes for what feels like an eternity because my tears keep falling, and I have to blink them away several times to see him. "I love you." His voice is clear and deep and commanding. His eyes are questioning.

I gasp once, a breath in and out like when he lands a new mark purposefully over a fresh welt to deepen my need for him. "I love you." My voice is strong and soft and giving. My eyes are his answer.

I never would've had the strength to say these words without Them. I never would've known their true meaning without Simon.

Because what I had before…what Grace and I and the others had before…the memory of the library and bittersweet moments of tenderness…all of that is nothing compared to this. This is just us. Simon and me. Raw and exposed.

And it's perfect that I'm naked, that he's naked, and that I'm tied to his bed and at his mercy because I trust him, like I've trusted no other. He is my Trust. My heart. My love.

And I'm everything to him, everything he's needed. I've known his feelings for me since he took Miles away. Only a man determined in his love would do what he's done for me.

He pulls my face to him, and I strain against the rope to reach him more. When his teeth finally stop biting my lips and his tongue finally stops reaching for mine, he doesn't let my face go. He again looks quickly between my eyes, and I sense his difference, taking a breath in that I hold until my stretched ribs burn along with the ache between my legs.

"I need you, Red."

"I know, Trust. You have me." I smile, sweet and slow. I'm lost in a memory of the number of times we've been here before. My body aches, even as my heart feels a guilt for all that he's given me, done for me.

I whisper what he needs to hear, the softness of what was best about Grace in my voice, "Hurt me like you've had to hurt him, baby…I can take it…"

A match strikes in his eyes. The mention of Miles is enough to do that. Simon leans back, looking at me more intensely. He seems to come to some decision. His grin darkens. "Oh no, sweetheart, one has nothing to do with the other."

He won't let me go to the cave where he holds Miles. He won't let me see what he does to break the man that tried to break me. Simon won't say anything about his debt to his cousin for helping in all this either. I know he doesn't let Cary do much; I've heard them arguing enough to know this.

But I know that he needs me as much as he needs the cock-hardening pills to get him through what he must do. It was his plan, and only he would have the strength to see it to the end. For me. But I'd gladly bear this guilt if I could take his pain away and make it my own instead.

He brushes my hair away from my cheek, cupping my face again and putting his thumb in between my open lips. I try to smile around him, even as he pushes deeper into my mouth, scraping himself against my teeth, in and out. "I talked to Cary. He ratted you out."

I frown but can't move with Simon's thumb pinning me to the pillow. I try for a mischievous grin, as much as I can. He laughs, a teasing chuckle that shoots a need straight to my drenched crotch. "He said there were some silly thoughts going on in that pretty head of yours."

My stomach drops for a moment, and I mentally curse Cary for his big mouth. I tried last week to get information out of his cousin, even though Simon made it clear that Cary was on express orders to ignore any efforts I'd make. I know this has to be hard for Simon, and I only wanted to get some nugget of detail that I might use to comfort him more. Cary didn't tell me anything, even after I answered his question about my reason for wanting to know.

I frown at Simon and try to say, "damn snitch," but it comes out sounding like spit and gibberish with his thumb still firmly hooked in my mouth. I start to bite down, and Simon only laughs, "Go for it." I stop.

"Gigi." He sighs, a heavy-hearted sound that makes me ache all over. Unfamiliar tears spring to my eyes in response. "Stop that." He pulls his thumb out and gives me a light smack on my cheek. I blink the tears away. "That's better. Stop thinking you know what I'm going to say before I say it." I nod, uncertain because I know damn well what he's going to say. He's doing all this for me. I stay silent though. I am tied up after all.

"Gigi, I've done a lot of things in my life that others—other men—wouldn't be proud of. But *I* am. The only thing that I've regretted is letting you slip through my fingers. Twice." He gives me a menacing smile now with one eyebrow raised, his thumb tracing over my lips. "I don't regret *anything* else. And I *won't* regret it. Ever. Not so long as I have you."

I swallow and whisper against his thumb, "You have me."

"Then stop pissing me off with feeling guilty about what *I've* decided to do for us. *You* had no choices, Red, but *I* did. This was *my* decision, and I'd make it again. *For us*." I swallow harder, readying to argue. "Open those gorgeous lips to say anything besides 'yes sire,' and you'll be spending the week I'm gone in the cave."

I laugh at this, kissing his thumb. I know he's bluffing. He already started work on reverting the land back to a proper vineyard, Trust Red Winery. The cave will be the perfect spot for storage and barrel tastings. Full renovations will start the day after he leaves. I mockingly say, "Yes, Sire," giggling more as his palm presses down on my lips.

"You're going to pay for that brattiness." He looks down at his cock, still standing straight up and engorged, as he gets to his feet. I know he has hours of this torment, and I want all of it to be mine.

Our needs are matched, as they always have been, and I smile. "Yes, please." I can see in his eyes that did it. He's a sucker when I beg for it, but I just have to add, "Sire," to wickedly motivate him properly.

He chuckles. "We'll go for a swim when I'm done." Sliding the crop off me, I watch as he returns it to the cabinet and selects a thick, leather paddle instead.

"I'd like that." I know that the pool is cleansing for him, and it reminds me of the stillness I now have in my head. It's good for us both to float and laugh and just be…but that will come later. After we release some of our demons, we'll float in waves we create together.

My attention is drawn from thoughts of serenity. Simon stands over me with the paddle held high and a gleam in his eyes. "Turn over." There's no denying the demand in his voice.

There's enough slack in the rope to allow me to twist my arms. Wrists crossing, I flip over onto my stomach and tremble in anticipation.

And I know this image…of my body stretched and waiting, with light marks from yesterday still healing…this will be what Simon imagines when he heads back to the cave tomorrow, back to deal with Miles, back to finish what he's started.

The image of my body writhing with his blows, keening up to meet them…this is what I give to him freely as he finally frees me from my past once and for all. And it's what I'll imagine, tied again to this same spot, waiting for his return to me, to our love. My Trust. My Simon. My match.

All thoughts of guilt or a cave are long gone with the first thud of the paddle, centered and hard. The thwack is solid and frightening in the quietness of our bedroom. My ass wobbles with it. I know I'll have bruises tomorrow. I let out a small, high hiss and wait for more. I just love when he doesn't build up to heavier hits but starts right at the top of my threshold.

He grunts, and I don't tense as two more sound thwacks land quickly. He rarely uses the paddle. He prefers the whip or cane; I think it's the sound and artistry he can achieve with them that he likes more.

Thwack. I hum through a deep breath out, spreading my legs more and lifting up for him. He can't resist the invitation and gets a squeal out of me by biting on my right cheek hard. I have the image of me as the apple and him as the serpent, and I giggle as he lands two more hits, cutting it off to a low groan. I moan through the rest, trying to rise again to meet him.

Thwack. Thwack. He's panting with the full-body swings. I know he needs the physical release of this; that's why he's not using the whip. Thwack.

I'm almost there, almost at the point when I need to withdraw a little from the pain, but I wait just a little longer. Three more hits, and I feel the warmth spreading into a numbness. He pauses, and I tilt my head back, my hair covering my face, sweat plastering it to me.

He's panting harder, but the paddle is still clutched in his hand. Our eyes lock, and he smiles a little. I smile back and mouth, "More." He doesn't hesitate in giving me what I want, what he needs. I lose track of the lift and fall of his arm, the sound of leather on my flesh and our moans perfectly in sync.

When he stops, we're both drenched in sweat. He's on the bed quickly; his hot hands pull my legs apart and lift my hips up. I feel his hard cock press between my swollen and tender cheeks, and I press back to him so his length slides up and down my crack.

He laughs, "I think I've had enough ass for today, sweetheart." And he lowers himself in between my lips. My laugh is cut off as he enters me quickly in one long, smooth push. I squeeze him and tilt my hips to pull him in deeper, to push him against my wall. His hot, sweaty chest leans over my hot, sweaty back, and his fingers cup around me, finding my swollen clit and forcing another squeal out of me.

We ride each other this way, not much in and out, more deep pressing and pulling. When we come together, we're both moaning guttural sounds that I can feel between my legs.

He stretches us out, flattening his body over mine, and I love the feel of his weight. I love the feel of our bodies cooling together, our breathing slowing together. Just when I think he's asleep and I'll be stuck under him, he slowly moves just his lower half off me. I take a deep breath in and shudder when he traces his fingers in a light circle on my right shoulder.

"I'm going to carve my initials right here before I leave for Durban."

I turn my head to look at him, but he's busy now untying me. "Not a tattoo?" He shakes his head, still concentrating on the ropes. I laugh, "Isn't that a little primitive?"

Now that I'm free, he looks me right in the eyes, moving my hair off my face. "That's me, Red. Primitive."

And I smile…because I wouldn't want him any other way.

The author's debut series:

WILLOW MADISON

True Nature

TRUE SERIES BOOK 1

True Nature is the first book in a series that includes 2 alternative endings. It combines elements of Domestic Discipline, Dark Romance, and D/s. It's not a typical hearts and flowers story. There are thorns, and it's not for the faint-of-heart.

I know. I know.

How many times have you heard that? Me too.

I hate this part—the "warning" or "trigger" alert. I don't really know what to say. Because I don't really know you— the reader—I can't presume to know what emotions you'll go through with this series.

I can tell you that I had fun writing it. But I'm sick and twisted that way. In this series, I take a sweet, innocent girl (some may call my heroine a doormat...gah'head, Lucy doesn't mind) and let one helluva an Alpha try to twist her into his ultimate picture of perfection. I get tingly just thinking of all that happens to poor Lucy. But she doesn't mind this either. Oh no, Lucy doesn't mind at all. Maybe she's just as sick and twisted as me? Sorry, you can't see me, but I'm shrugging.

Max is my Hero. Well...anti-hero *is* a bit more accurate I suppose. Maybe you'll love him. Maybe you'll hate him. Maybe you'll love to hate him. Doesn't matter. Max knows he's a bastard, and he doesn't give a shit. He's found what he wants.

This is Lucy's and Max's story.

It *is* a love story—a merrily, sick and twisted love story.

On board with that? Cool. Enjoy the ride.

Made in the USA
San Bernardino, CA
16 March 2020